Dear Reader,

After watching two movies about single women inheriting children I started thinking. What would happen if two people, a couple, inherited a baby and were totally unprepared for their new responsibility?

My own experience provided the backstory. Until I got pregnant, I didn't think much about what would happen if my husband and I died. But with a baby on the way, we realized it was time to write our wills. My newborn daughter's first outing was to the attorney's office. Sometimes being a writer means it's all too easy to imagine the worst. So along with the will, I wrote a letter detailing my dreams for our daughter. I even suggested future birthday presents!

Death is never an easy topic to write about, especially in a romance novel, but love brings light to even the darkest times. Love can overcome the obstacles in our way and heal our wounded hearts. Even after we are no longer here, love remains. Constant and strong. Forever.

I hope Kate and Jared's lessons in love as they form a new family with baby Cassidy warms your heart as much as it did mine.

Enjoy!

Melissa McClone

Kate wasn't about to allow Jared back into her life, into her bed, into her heart only to watch him leave and hurt her again. Unless...

She thought about her wedding rings locked away in a safety deposit box at her bank. She never thought she would put the gold band and diamond solitaire back on her finger. Her heart pounded.

"Things would have to be very different," she said, formulating the plan in her head.

Jared eyed her warily. "What do you have in mind?"

Kate couldn't believe she was considering this, but she had no other choice if she wanted to keep Cassidy. And that was what she wanted. More than anything. She rubbed her thumb over her bare ring finger. "A marriage of convenience."

His brows furrowed. "A what?"

"A marriage in name only for Cassidy's sake."

A nerve throbbed in Jared's neck. "You'd go for that kind of marriage?"

She inhaled sharply. Logically she knew that kind of marriage would work. Emotionally.... No, she wasn't going there.

"I would." This was the best solution for everyone involved. "How about you? Would you agree to a marriage of convenience?"

MELISSA McCLONE

Marriage for Baby

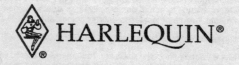

HARLEQUIN®

TORONTO • NEW YORK • LONDON
AMSTERDAM • PARIS • SYDNEY • HAMBURG
STOCKHOLM • ATHENS • TOKYO • MILAN • MADRID
PRAGUE • WARSAW • BUDAPEST • AUCKLAND

ISBN-13: 978-0-373-03947-0
ISBN-10:   0-373-03947-6

MARRIAGE FOR BABY

First North American Publication 2007.

With a degree in mechanical engineering from Stanford University, the last thing **Melissa McClone** ever thought she would be doing was writing romance novels. But analyzing engines for a major U.S. airline just couldn't compete with her "happily-ever-afters." When she isn't writing, caring for her three young children or doing laundry, Melissa loves to curl up on the couch with a cup of tea, her cats and a good book. She enjoys watching home-decorating shows to get ideas for her house—a 1939 cottage that is *slowly* being renovated. Melissa lives in Lake Oswego, Oregon, with her own real-life hero husband, two daughters, a son, two lovable but oh-so-spoiled indoor cats and a no-longer-stray outdoor kitty that decided to call the garage home. Melissa loves to hear from her readers. You can write to her at P.O. Box 63, Lake Oswego, OR 97034, U.S.A.

Melissa McClone on *Marriage for Baby:*

"When I had to attend a romance writers' conference—four-month-old baby in tow!— my husband gallantly stepped in, caring for baby Mackenna during my days of workshops and meetings. One morning as I waved to them across the crowded hotel lobby, I thought the baby looked a little...odd. Just like my hero, Jared, my husband had dressed our daughter with clothing on backwards! I laughed it off and explained to her daddy that tags go in the back."

For Virginia Kantra and Tiffany Talbott,
talented writers and friends extraordinaire.
Special thanks to Ceci and Robert Kramer.

CHAPTER ONE

STANDING on the sidewalk outside the lawyer's office, Kate Malone stared at the double glass doors. She still had a few minutes until her appointment. No reason to rush inside.

She raised her face to the cloudless, blue sky. The spring sunshine heated her cheeks. Sun kisses. That's what Susan called them.

Susan.

The unusually warm April temperature reminded Kate of their college graduation eight years ago. She had approached the proceedings as a necessary step, one more thing to mark off her To Do List on the way to the top, but not her best friend, Susan. Unlike Kate, Susan had relished every moment of the drawn-out ceremony in the sweltering ninety-degree heat. She'd bounced across the stage, tossed her University of Oregon diploma box in the air and twirled around.

A smiled tugged on Kate's lips. Susan always lived life to the fullest. Or rather...

Had lived.

Until a driver fell asleep at the wheel and collided head-on with Susan's car two days ago here in Boise, Idaho.

Tears stung Kate's eyes. Grief slashed through her. How could Susan be dead? Susan, so full of life, so full of love. Susan, with her adoring husband, Brady, and their cute baby, Cassidy...

All three had died in the crash.

Kate swallowed, hard.

No. She couldn't lose control now.

She didn't have a tissue. Or the time.

She needed to hold herself together during the meeting with Susan and Brady's attorney. Once Kate checked into her hotel, she could fall apart, but not until then.

Squaring her shoulders, she pushed open one of the doors to the law office and stepped inside. A blast of cool air hit her. Goose bumps prickled on her arms. The sight of the empty receptionist desk deflated her resolve. Her composure slipped a notch. Now that she was inside, she wanted to get this over with.

"Kate?"

The familiar male voice made her stiffen. Jared. She wasn't ready to face him. Not now. Possibly not ever. And yet she found herself turning in the direction of his voice.

As Jared rose from a leather club chair, her breath caught in her throat. He wore a tailored gray suit and the multicolored silk tie she'd given him for his thirty-first birthday.

Five years ago when Brady and Susan had introduced them, Jared Reed had been a twenty-something single woman's fantasy. He'd gotten only more handsome. Kate's heart thudded. She wished she still didn't find him so attractive.

His square jaw and slightly crooked nose—from a snowboarding accident when he was a teenager—gave his face the right amount of rugged character to offset his long lashes and lush lips. She couldn't believe how much his hair had grown in the last three months. Normally he went for the short, corporate cut, but the wavy, carefree style suited him better.

Not that she cared.

Much.

His hazel-green eyes met hers. "How are you?"

"I-I'm—" Her voice cracked. Tears blurred her vision. Oh, no. She didn't want him to see her like this.

Kate blinked. Once, twice.

"I'm so sorry, Katie." He was at her side in an instant and brushed his lips across her forehead. "So very sorry."

At the best of times, she struggled to remain indifferent to him, but his tender gesture and simple, yet sincere words shattered her defenses. She sunk against him, breathing in his familiar soap and water scent, drawing in the welcome comfort of his hard chest.

Stop…now, logic shouted.

Get away…now, common sense cried.

But Kate didn't want to listen. She didn't care if her actions went against rational thought. Jared understood what she was going through. He was going through the same thing.

"I'm sorry, too," she choked out. "It's so…"

He wrapped his arms around her. "Horrible."

She hugged him. "I keep thinking it's a mistake or I'm going to wake up and it's all been a bad dream."

"Me, too," he admitted. "As soon as I heard, I called your office. They said you were out of town."

"Boston."

"I didn't want to leave a message."

"I wouldn't have gotten it." She closed her eyes. Not being alone felt so good. "After my assistant phoned me with the news, I turned off my phone."

"A first."

"I hope I never have to do it again."

He gave her shoulder a reassuring squeeze. "So do I."

She stared at him. "I'm sorry I didn't think to call you."

"You wouldn't have been able to reach me. I was in San Francisco. My boss had me pulled out of a meeting and relayed the message." A corner of Jared's mouth lifted. "Besides, I didn't expect you to call, Kate."

She flinched. "Why not? Brady was your best friend."

"Susan was like a sister to you. How old were you when you met?

"Seven." In a foster home. Kate's first. Susan's third. That had been so long ago. They had come so far.

"Seven," he repeated. "You have to be devastated."

Devastated didn't begin to describe the anguish ripping Kate apart. She felt as if a part of her had died, too. She inhaled slowly.

Jared's arms tightened around her, and she found herself resting her head against his chest, a foreign yet familiar position. "It's okay to cry, Katie."

She fought the urge to pull away. But she couldn't. Not when she relished the feel of him, of the steady beat of his heart beneath her cheek.

"I've cried." Kate didn't want to sound defensive. It was the truth. She had cried. More than she would ever admit. She just didn't like crying in front of others.

"I spoke to Brady a couple of weeks ago," Jared said.

"Susan e-mailed me a picture of Cassidy on Thursday. She promised to send more." But those pictures would never arrive. The baby girl would never grow any bigger. Kate smothered a sob. "I can't believe they're gone. Why them? Why now?"

"I wish I knew."

"Me, too."

But thinking about what she'd lost hurt so much. Too much. She'd rather think about something else. Someone else. Jared.

Kate curled the ends of his hair with her finger. It had never been long enough to do this before, and she liked the extra length. He brushed his hand through her hair, his fingers sifting through the strands, the way he always had. She nearly sighed.

It was as if nothing had changed between them. Kate knew that wasn't true, but she wasn't ready to back out of his arms.

For now she could pretend the past didn't matter and ignore the future. She could do that because she needed Jared. She needed his warmth, his strength, him. And a part of her hoped he needed her, too.

He cupped her face with his left hand. She noticed the gold band on his fourth finger. Her ring finger felt conspicuously bare. She curled her hand into a fist.

"Mr. and Mrs. Reed?" a female voice asked.

Jared turned his head. "Yes?"

A cute brunette with short, curly hair and dangling gold earrings stood next to the receptionist's desk.

Kate backed out of his embrace. "Actually I'm—"

"My wife. Kate Malone," he interrupted, a slight edge to his voice. "I'm Jared Reed."

Kate recalled the long discussions about her not taking his name. He had claimed to understand, to accept her decision. But he hadn't. Not really. She shifted uncomfortably.

"I'm sorry, Ms. Malone. Mr. Reed." The woman picked up a thick manila file from the receptionist's desk. "Don Phillips is running a few minutes late. I'll show you to his office once I drop off this folder."

"Thank you," Jared said.

As the woman walked away, Kate bit her lip. "Why didn't you tell her the truth?"

"Because with or without your wedding band, you are still my wife." His gaze hardened. "At least until the divorce is finalized."

The receptionist led them down a hallway and motioned to an office at the end. "Don will be right with you."

"Thanks." Jared hoped the atmosphere in the office would be more comfortable than that of the lobby. But knowing Kate, he wasn't going to hold his breath.

The woman smiled. "Let me know if you need anything."

"We will." He was tempted to ask the friendly receptionist to stay until the lawyer joined them. That might ease the tension between him and Kate. Not to mention the silence. Kate hadn't spoken to him since he'd mentioned the word divorce. His jaw clamped. Maybe she'd forgotten she was the one who filed.

No. That wasn't fair.

She'd lost her best friend and goddaughter. She was in tremendous pain. Who knew what was going through her beautiful, blond head?

Kate sat in one of the chairs opposite a large mahogany desk. With a posture that would make a charm school proud, she looked poised and in control as she studied the diploma hanging behind the desk. Not surprising really. Kate kept her emotions under a tight lid, and hated showing any sign of weakness.

Or at least had until today when she entered the law office on the verge of tears. She had looked so lost and alone. The sadness on her face had clawed at his heart.

Jared sat in the chair next to her and extended his hand. "You okay?"

She nodded once, not meeting his gaze. Maybe she didn't see his hand, either.

At least he'd tried. Jared rested his arm on the chair. No one could say he hadn't tried to save his marriage or hadn't wanted to give the relationship another go. He had, and he would. If she would give him the chance.

Ironic, Jared thought. Brady and Susan had introduced him to Kate. Now their deaths were bringing them back together after almost three months apart.

The seconds turned into minutes. The only sound was the ticking of a vintage Felix the Cat clock. At least one thing hadn't changed since the last time he saw Kate. The same stone-cold silence. They had been in Boise three months ago for Cassidy's baptism. The weekend hadn't gone well. Separation and divorce had been mentioned, but he hadn't expected the call from her lawyer the next week. Ever since then lawyers had handled the communication between them. And that seemed…strange. Wrong. Yet Kate wouldn't consider another option. He brushed his hand through his hair. "Kate—"

"There's a reason I'm not wearing my wedding rings."

Uh-oh. Jared drew a cautious breath. Words and actions could easily be misconstrued with emotions running so high. He and Kate were both hurting enough, but he couldn't deny how seeing her ringless finger had affected him. "You don't owe me any explanations."

"I was afraid the ring would fall off," she said anyway, still not meeting his eyes. "I lost some weight."

More than "some" by the way she'd felt in his arms. She'd felt thinner, fragile. He'd chalked it up to grief. Now he wasn't so sure.

Kate never went out without looking perfect—hair, makeup, clothing. She called it the "whole package", even though she looked as beautiful to him in ratty, old sweats, a stained T-shirt and ponytail. Today, however, Kate looked as if she'd had to work harder on the package. And he could see the difference.

The energetic, multitasking dynamo, who owned one of the hottest and fastest growing public relation firms in the Pacific Northwest, had all but disappeared. Jared expected to see Kate's normally bright blue eyes red and swollen given the circumstances, but not so wary, stressed, exhausted. Her sunken cheeks and loose fitting designer clothes went beyond grief, and the changes worried him.

"You need to remember to eat," he said.

"I eat."

He raised an eyebrow.

She set her chin. "I just forget sometimes."

Most of the time. Jared used to text message her at lunchtime and dinnertime. Now that he wasn't around to remind her, she probably didn't bother to eat a decent meal. "You should schedule food into your day."

"I do," she said, a little too quickly. "Do you?"

"I don't need to. I enjoy food too much to skip meals."

"I don't skip meals. I forget." Her mouth twitched. "I don't want to argue."

She never did anymore. The only place Jared had seen Kate really lose control was in bed. "We're not arguing."

"Just drop it. Okay?"

He checked the time. The second hand moved slower than his niece's turtle, Corky.

"Sorry to keep you waiting." A middle-aged man, wearing a tailored navy suit and wire-rimmed glasses, burst into the office. "I'm Don Phillips, the Lukas's attorney."

Jared rose and shook the man's hand. "Jared Reed."

Kate remained seated. "Kate Malone."

The lawyer sat behind his desk, and Jared sat, too.

"I'm so sorry for the loss of your friends," Don said. "It's such a tragedy."

Jared nodded. Kate placed her clasped hands on her lap.

"Thank you for coming so quickly." Don reached for a file. "I'd hoped to speak with you personally when I called yesterday, but under the circumstances I felt it was imperative to get you to Boise as soon as possible."

"We understand," Jared said. "Have funeral arrangements been made?"

"Yes." Don pulled out a piece of paper from the file. "Mr. Lukas, Brady's father, took care of that. A vigil will be held at the funeral home on Wednesday and a memorial service on Thursday. The church will put on a reception in the hall afterward. Then the bodies will be flown to Maine for burial."

The lawyer made it sound so easy like a checklist.

"Susan…" Kate's voice trailed off.

"What?" Jared asked.

"It's just—" she tucked her hair behind her ears "—Susan never really liked Maine."

"No, she didn't," Don agreed. "But she and Brady had their burial location put in their wills."

"Oh." Kate wet her lips. "Okay, then."

"A situation like this is never easy, but fortunately Brady and Susan had the foresight to plan for such an occurrence."

Occurrence? A chill inched down Jared's spine. Perhaps that was legalese for death. Either way, all of this was difficult for him to hear.

"No amount of planning will make this any easier to deal with, but logistically, having wills in place will make things proceed a little smoother." Don pulled out a thick document from the file. "I attended the same church as Brady and Susan, and I drew up their wills. Since they had no family in town, I kept the originals here in the office."

"Shouldn't we wait for Brady's parents?" Jared asked.

"Mr. and Mrs. Lukas aren't coming," Don explained. "Although Mr. Lukas handled the funeral arrangements, their doctors felt the trip from the East Coast would be too much for them with their current health conditions. They received copies of both wills after they were written so they know, and agree with, what their son and daughter-in-law decided. May I proceed?"

Jared nodded. He watched for Kate's reaction, but she held herself together tightly. This had to be tearing her up inside, and he ignored the urge to touch her.

"As you know, Brady was an only child and Susan had been in foster homes since she was five. They had no living relatives other than Brady's parents." Don's gaze rested on Kate. "Though Susan considered you more a sister than a friend."

Kate's composed façade cracked for an instant. "I felt the same way."

"The Lukases thought highly of you, Jared," Don said. "Brady and Susan each named you their personal representative to handle their estates. Do you accept their nominations?"

Jared had no idea what sort of responsibilities would be involved as Brady and Susan's executor, but that didn't matter. "I'm honored and happy to accept. May I retain your services? I've never done something like this before so I will need your expertise."

"I'll gladly counsel and offer you assistance. The sooner we get started, the better. I would like to submit the wills and obtain your appointment as personal representative through informal proceedings. That way a hearing won't be required."

Proceedings. Hearing. Jared's muscles tensed. This was too weird. A few weeks ago he'd been making plans to attend a poker tournament with Brady while Kate spent the weekend with Susan. Now he was overseeing their friends' probate.

As Don scribbled notes on a yellow legal pad, Jared glanced at Kate. She acted like this was nothing more than another one of the endless meetings she attended, but he noticed her hands trembling. He wanted to pull her onto his lap and hold her until she felt better, until she smiled again.

"Once you're officially appointed their personal representative, you'll want to call a locksmith and have the locks changed on the Lukas's residence," Don said. "I can provide recommendations."

"I'd appreciate the referrals," Jared said.

"Why do the locks need to be changed?" Kate asked.

"We don't know who might have keys to the house," Don explained. "Baby-sitters, neighbors, housecleaners. The list goes on. You don't want to chance a robbery. Unfortunately such break-ins have occurred."

Jared pictured the two-story house Brady and Susan called home. The couple had been too busy working on the nursery to fix up the rest of the house. Now that task would fall to the new owner. Jared thought of his and Kate's home, the hours they'd spent working on the old house. Kissing on a ladder. Making love on a drop cloth. Kate obsessing over paint chips. That seemed like so long ago.

Soon the house would be hers. He hadn't fought Kate for it, even though he loved the home with all its creaks, foibles and bad plumbing. But his life was no longer in Portland. His life was no longer with Kate. He kept telling himself that, even though the words never seemed to make things easier. And he'd yet to fully believe them.

"Do I have your permission to proceed?" Don asked.

"Please do," Jared said, grateful for the lawyer's help.

Don shuffled papers. "And now Cassidy."

Kate's befuddlement matched Jared's confusion. "What about Cassidy?" he asked.

"You and Kate have been nominated for joint guardianship in both wills," Don said, but his words made no sense. "You realize, of course, you are under no legal obligation to accept the guardian appointment."

Kate's lower lip quivered. "I don't understand."

Neither did Jared. Guardian? Of Cassidy? But...

He shook his head. "There has to be some mistake."

"I suggest clients discuss guardianship with prospective nominees before naming them in their wills," Don added. "Otherwise the nomination can come as a shock."

Shock didn't come close to what Jared was feeling. "You don't understand—"

"They discussed it with us." Kate's voice sounded hoarse, unnatural. "But Cassidy is dead."

The lawyer frowned.

Jared reached for her hand and laced his fingers with hers. "The message I received said the family had been in an accident and the Lukas's were dead."

"I was told the same," Kate said.

"Oh, no. There's been some sort of miscommunication." Don's face went grim. "Cassidy was in the accident, but she survived."

Kate clung to Jared's hand. He understood how she felt, afraid to hope, afraid to believe the news could be true, because the letdown would be even worse.

"She's alive?" Kate whispered.

Jared held his breath.

"Cassidy is very much alive." Don set his pen on the desk. "She's at the hospital recovering from her injuries."

Thank God. An enormous weight lifted from Jared's shoulders. He knew how much Brady loved his baby girl, how much Brady would have wanted her to go on with or without him.

Kate jumped up from her chair, pulling Jared with her.

Tears streamed down her face. She smiled at him. An almost forgotten warmth seeped into his heart. "I can't believe it."

He smiled back. "Believe it."

She hugged him. The scent of her shampoo—grapefruit—filled his nostrils. Her mane of hair brushed against him and he remembered how much he'd miss holding her and touching her and loving her.

"Is it wrong to feel happy?" she whispered, her warm breath caressed his neck.

"It's fine, Kate." Jared held onto her. "I feel the same way."

They both laughed, a sound he never thought he'd hear in the near future let alone today.

"I am so sorry." Don removed his glasses and rubbed his eyes. "It was a difficult day yesterday. I thought I was clear on the phone but perhaps I wasn't."

"Cassidy's alive." Kate sat, but didn't let go of Jared's hand so he sat, too. "That's what matters. Is she okay?"

"Cassidy is in stable condition," Don explained. "The car seat seems to have protected her from more serious injuries."

Kate sucked in a breath. Jared blew his out.

"What?" Don asked.

"Our baby shower gift was the car seat," Jared said.

Don leaned forward. "Excellent gift."

Jared nodded, but he felt strange. Kate had spent hours poring over catalogs and reading car seat reviews in order to pick the right one. He'd thought she was being obsessive again, but her research could have saved the baby's life.

Her lips parted. Was she remembering?

How could she not? Cassidy was alive. Her parents were dead. And the little girl belonged to him and Kate.

Jared remembered when Brady and Susan had flown in for a weekend. Susan and Kate had spent the day shopping for maternity clothes while Brady helped Jared build a trellis for the yard. That night over a bottle of sparkling cider, Brady and Susan asked them to be the baby's guardians. They told them to think about the request. Jared and Kate did and agreed the next morning.

But that was before. Before the separation. Before Kate had filed for divorce.

"How recent is the will?" Jared asked.

"I met with Brady and Susan a week after Cassidy was born." Don got a faraway look in his eyes. "I remember them telling me this was the baby's first outing since coming home from the hospital. Susan said she'd put it into the baby book."

That didn't make sense. Brady and Susan would have known about the marriage problems, about Jared living and working in Seattle and Kate in Portland. Something wasn't adding up.

"What's the problem?" Kate asked. "We told them we would do it."

"This is a life-changing decision," Don said. "Don't rush. You have thirty days after we start guardianship proceedings to accept the appointment."

"We're not declining," she said.

Jared agreed with her. Of course he did. But he needed to be sure this was what his friends wanted for their daughter. Guardians with a disintegrating, soon-to-be-over marriage didn't seem like the number one choice parents would make. "Could you please read the guardianship portion of the will?"

Don paged through the paperwork. "Since Brady and Susan wanted to name both of you as guardians, I suggested additional wording to the wills, which they agreed to."

That made sense to Jared, and he wanted to hear the

wording. Especially since Brady and Susan knew about the marriage problems.

"Here's the passage from Brady's will. Susan's is identical." The lawyer put on his glasses. "'If my spouse does not survive me and if at the time of my death any of my children are minors or under a legal disability, I appoint Jared Reed and Kate Malone to act jointly as the guardian of each child who is a minor or under a legal disability so long as Jared Reed and Kate Reed are both then living and married on the date of such appointment.'"

Kate straightened in her chair.

Jared felt her tension. It wasn't so bad, though. They were living. They were still married. They were fine.

At least as far as the baby was concerned.

Of course Cassidy would become part of the divorce settlement. No doubt Susan would want Kate to have custody.

"Are there any provisions if our marriage ends at a future date?" Kate asked, her voice cool.

"Actually there is. Again both wills contain the same wording." Don flipped the page. "'If Jared Reed and Kate Malone are not married to each other on the date of such appointment or become separated or divorced at a later date, I appoint Jared Reed to solely act as the guardian of each child of mine who is a minor or under a legal disability.'"

"What?" Kate asked.

Jared sat stunned. "Me?"

CHAPTER TWO

KATE'S heart pounded. Every muscle tensed. She didn't believe her ears.

She couldn't.

"There must be some mistake." Her gaze darted between a shell-shocked Jared and a contemplative Don. "Susan would never have agreed to that."

"It's not a mistake," Don said matter-of-factly as if they were discussing the custody of a pampered pet not Kate's precious goddaughter. "Brady and Susan were clear with their wishes and made sure I understood them."

Kate flexed her fingers, fighting to grasp the situation. Fighting for control. "But it makes no sense."

"I agree." Jared's confident voice reassured her. "I may have been nominated as the personal representative, but the sole guardian? Kate and Susan were as close as sisters. There's no reason I should be the one named in the wills."

Relief and gratitude washed over Kate. Thank goodness he understood how ridiculous this was. No doubt Jared would support her in getting this overturned.

His gaze met hers. They were on the same side for once. And that felt…good. Satisfying. In a way it hadn't for a very long time.

"Remember that's only if you and Kate divorce," Don added. "As long as you are together, the provision doesn't apply."

Her relief ebbed.

The split of assets had been agreed upon; the paperwork had been filed. It was only a matter of time, weeks really, until the divorce was official.

Panic threatened. Kate grabbed onto the chair. She couldn't lose control.

Not when she had to think. Kate needed to figure out a way to fix this. First, they had to be named guardians. Together. Then she and Jared could challenge the validity of the will so she could gain sole guardianship of Cassidy. Of course, Jared would have whatever visitation rights he wanted.

She eased her death grip on the chair arms. Now that she had a plan formulated, she could cope.

"If it's any consolation, Kate," Don said, his voice startling her. "You are named sole guardian if Jared dies."

"Don't give her any ideas."

His wry humor reminded Kate of the time he playfully accused her of poisoning him when she made juice using organic kale, rhubarb and strawberries after a trip to the Farmer's Market. A smile pulled at her mouth. She caught herself. This wasn't the time for fun. She pressed her lips together.

"What happens next?" Jared asked the lawyer.

"Well, since you're married you will both receive guardianship if you accept the nomination," Don explained. "But I'm sure this is something you want to discuss in private. No guardian can be named until the personal representative is officially appointed and the wills submitted for probate."

She struggled to make sense of his words, to understand their implications. "What about Cassidy? What happens to her in the meanwhile?

"Cassidy is currently under state custody," Don said.

That was one thing Kate understood all too well. "No. Susan would not have wanted that for her baby."

"But since Cassidy's in the hospital, she won't be put into a foster home, correct?" Jared asked.

"Yes, as long as guardianship has been determined by her release," Don said. "If we run into any snags, we can petition to have a temporary guardian named until final guardianship is determined."

Jared covered Kate's hand with his. "We'll make sure there aren't any snags."

She fought the urge to hug him. With everything they'd been through these past months, she'd forgotten Jared Reed was still a good guy. His reassurance meant so much.

Kate stole a glance at him, and he winked. Her pulse quickened. She mouthed the word thanks and looked away. As fast as she could without seeming rude. Gratefulness. That was all her reaction was, all it ever could be.

"Susan and Brady left letters for you." Don handed Kate a large, thick manila envelope, and Jared received a thin, standard business-size one. "Would you like to read them now or later?"

She clutched the envelope as if it were a winning Powerball lottery ticket. A part of her was afraid to look inside, but the other part wanted to rip the flap off and start reading. "Now."

"Later," Jared said at the same time.

Deadlock. They never could agree on anything. At first their differences had been a joke, and they'd laughed about it. Over and over again. But their disagreements had been a sign. Even though she might have loved Jared, even though she might sometimes long for him, they didn't work well together.

"You can open yours later," she said. "I'd prefer to open mine now."

Jared ran his finger under the flap of the envelope. "Now is fine."

Don rose from the desk. "I'll get the paperwork started."

Kate mumbled a thank you. As she focused on the envelope in her hand, she heard paper crinkle and unfold and a chuckle.

With trembling fingers, she opened the manila envelope and pulled out several typed pages.

Dear Kate,

If you're reading this, I'm dead and it's a good thing I decided to write everything down for you. Brady thinks I'm being morbid, but until I had Cassidy I didn't give much thought to what would happen if I weren't here. And now in the middle of all this estate planning, I've been thinking about it too much.

The corners of Kate's mouthed curved. That was so like Susan. She thought about things too much. As did Kate. Obsessive? Perhaps. But she and Susan had called it ana-lytical thinking.

By now, Don Phillips has told you that we want you and Jared to raise Cassidy. This should come as no surprise. What would come as a shock is if Don told you that Jared would gain custody of

Cassidy if the two of you divorced. I know you're confused and mad at me.

Kate wasn't mad. How about stunned? Hurt? Bewildered? Betrayed? Her gaze strayed to Jared before returning to the letter.

My hope is you and Jared have resolved things by the time of our untimely and unfortunate demise (gotta love that phrase!) and are living happily ever after. You are truly meant for each other.

Oh, Susan. She was such an optimist. Even under the most horrible situations growing up, she had never stopped believing her life would improve. No matter what the odds. But this dream of Susan's wasn't in the cards for Kate.

And that realization hurt. Badly.

She had wanted a family with Jared, but the timing always seemed off. They spent so little time together with their jobs. He wanted her to have a baby right when her company took off. And then he asked her to give up everything she'd put her heart and soul into and move to Seattle. When she wouldn't do what he wanted, he left without her. Kate squeezed her eyes shut, but that didn't stop the memories or erase the pain.

"Here," Jared said.

She opened her eyes. He held a tissue out to her. She wasn't sure if his offer was out of compassion or pity. She didn't want him to think she was weak. Kate stiffened. "I don't need it."

"Just in case."

His half smile unfurled warmth inside her. And made her feel like an idiot. Jared was only trying to help her, not point out her weaknesses. She had to stop thinking of him as the enemy. Kate took the tissue. "Thank you."

"You're welcome."

His dark eyes seemed to see right through her, to her secret thoughts and feelings.

Heat. Fire. Passion.

Kate forced herself to breathe.

Okay, some sort of volatile chemistry remained between them. She'd go so far as to admit her physical attraction to Jared had increased during their separation.

No big deal.

A marriage couldn't survive on desire alone. She'd learned that lesson. She looked away.

"Are you finished?" Jared asked.

"No."

"I've read mine three times."

Did the letter mention her? Old inadequacies floated to the surface. Had Brady questioned her ability to care for Cassidy? Kate bit the inside of her cheek.

"What did the letter say?" she asked.

Jared smiled. "Typical Brady stuff that helps."

"I'm glad." She only hoped hers helped, too. Up until now, Susan's letter hadn't. "I need to finish mine."

"Go ahead."

Kate read how proud Susan was over Kate's accomplishments, their friendship and their love for one another. As she continued, the paper shook and Kate realized her hands were trembling.

> You and I know family doesn't have to mean blood relation, and that's what I'm counting on

because I want Cassidy to experience what being part of a loving family is all about. Jared with the crazy, meddlesome Reeds can provide that for her. She can have what we didn't have growing up. I need that for my child.

As tears streamed from Kate's eyes, she struggled to read the rest. She didn't like what Susan had written, but Kate understood and somehow that hurt more. Each word felt like a wound to her already aching heart. She fumbled for the tissue.

Jared handed her another one. She muttered thanks and wiped her eyes.

So much for challenging the will. She couldn't. Not when she knew what Susan wanted for her daughter. Kate would want the same for her own child. Wasn't that one reason she found Jared Reed with his large, supportive family so attractive when they'd first met? He'd had everything she hadn't had growing up.

But knowing the reasons and understanding them didn't make the circumstances any easier on her.

"Katie?" Jared placed his hand on her shoulder. The warmth of his touch nearly did her in, but she couldn't—didn't want to—pull away.

He and Cassidy were all Kate had left.

She dabbed her eyes with a tissue again. "I'm not finished."

Forgive me if I've written something that has hurt you. I'm only doing what I feel is best for my daughter. I love you, Katie. I always have and I always will.

Take care of my baby and love her the way we wanted to be loved!

Hugs and love,
Susan

She didn't want to let Susan down, but Kate didn't think that kind of love, the kind you didn't have to earn, was possible. Not any longer. But for her best friend, she would give it her all.

She traced Susan's name—the only word handwritten on the many pages—with her fingertip. Tears dropped onto the paper, and Kate dried them off. She didn't want the letter to be ruined. She wanted to keep it. For herself. For Cassidy.

Kate inhaled and exhaled slowly. Steady. Calm. In control. She squared her shoulders. With a steady gaze, she met Jared's inquisitive eyes. "They want you to have Cassidy."

"I know."

"It's…okay." Or would be. Someday. Somehow.

"I'm sorry."

"It's not your fault." No matter how much Kate would have liked to blame him for this, she couldn't. If only she knew what to do next. "I want to see Cassidy."

Jared nodded. "Let's sign whatever papers Don has prepared then go to the hospital."

The children's wing of the hospital was painted with bluebirds, colorful flowers and rainbows, but the cheery decor did nothing to ease Jared's growing anxiety. He'd been trying to come to terms with a divorce he didn't want and now he was about to become a guardian. A father.

A dad.

He thought about Brady's letter.

You've always wanted kids.

Jared had wanted to be a dad. After he and Kate first got married, she was enthusiastic about wanting kids, but they'd agreed to hold off for a couple of years to concentrate on their careers. Still he'd imagined having a family, the perfect family to go with his fantasy of the perfect marriage—two children, a fancy double stroller and a fully loaded minivan. But when Kate's company exploded onto the PR scene, she resisted starting a family. And then the Seattle opportunity arose. He thought the promotion and transfer was a way to have the family he desired, not destroy his marriage.

Divorce.

Jared hated that word. Divorce meant failure. He hated failing or losing at anything. But there didn't seem to be a damn thing he could do about it.

He was the first to admit they'd both made mistakes that contributed to the collapse of their marriage, but whereas Kate called the problems irreparable damage, Jared believed they could work through them. He missed Kate so much. If only she would get off the divorce kick and give their marriage a go…

Jared waited in the lobby for her. He would have preferred driving together, but she'd wanted a few minutes by herself. He didn't like her being alone when she was tired and stressed, but he understood. Their lives had been changed completely. Whatever the future held, however, they were in this together.

"Sorry." Kate's steps echoed on the tile floor. "I couldn't find a parking place."

Her red eyes suggested she'd been crying again. He wished she would let him help her get through this. "I just got here."

She adjusted the strap of her purse. "I hope Cassidy's okay."

"Don said she would be."

"I know, but there's okay and there's okay."

Her nervousness reminded him of the first time he invited her home to meet his family. She'd brought flowers and a bottle of wine. Kate had been pleasant, personable, perfect. He'd later discovered she'd bought a new outfit and had her hair done that day. Her efforts had touched him and taken their dating to a new level. Jared took her hand in his. "Let's find out how okay Cassidy is."

As they followed the yellow bricks painted on the floor and stepped onto the elevator hand in hand, he felt as if nothing had changed between them and they were still together. Still in love. Those had been the days.

He'd been attracted to Kate since the moment he first saw her, and that attraction had only grown once he realized her brain matched her beauty. They'd been a perfect match. The perfect couple.

He missed their conversations, even their disagreements. He missed everything about her from the sound of her laughter to the birthmark on her left shoulder. He especially missed the lovemaking. Their problems had never reached the bedroom. Yet somehow the marriage had gone wrong. Bad. But that didn't mean it was over. Maybe he could make something new, something good happen between them to show Kate they could still be together.

He stopped at the nurse's station. "I'm Jared Reed and this is Kate Malone. We're here to see Cassidy Lukas."

"I'm Rachel." The nurse smiled. "Don Phillips said you were on the way."

"How is she?" Kate asked.

"Cassidy is recovering well. She's in Room 402." The nurse picked up a file. "I'll make a note to have the doctor speak with you."

"Thank you," Kate said.

The small room had a chair in one corner, a sofa bed under a bank of windows and a strange looking crib against the far wall. The four-month-old baby girl slept oblivious to them or any of the machines connected to her. Cuts—some that had been stitched—and bruises—some purple, others yellow—covered her arms and face. A white bandage was wrapped around her head.

A wave of protectiveness washed over Jared. This baby was his and Kate's responsibility.

"She's so beautiful," Kate whispered with a hint of awe in her voice.

Seeing the compassion in her eyes as she stared at the baby triggered something deep within him. This—Kate, him and a baby—had been his dream.

She sighed. "Cassidy looks so much like Susan."

He saw the resemblance especially around the mouth and eyes. "But she's got Brady's chin. I hope that doesn't mean she's as stubborn as he was."

Kate smiled wanly. "Let's hope not."

He glanced around the room. A stuffed bear and a basket of flowers sat on a cart. He read the cards. The bear was from Don Phillips and his wife. The flowers from Brady's work.

Why wasn't the room full of flowers, balloons and cards? Where were all the visitors? Jared didn't get it. "Why is Cassidy all alone?"

"What do you mean?" Kate asked.

When his sister Heather gave birth to her third child, his family camped out in the waiting room. "There isn't anyone here with Cassidy. How come?"

"We're all she has."

"But friends. Surely Brady and Susan had some friends—"

"Who have their own families and lives," Kate explained. "Not everyone has a family like yours, Jared. A lot of people end up in the hospital alone. Even babies."

His mind accepted the truth of her words, but his heart and his upbringing rejected it. "That's not right."

"She won't have to be alone again. We can take shifts."

Shifts meant they wouldn't be together. He'd been apart from Kate for so long, too long, and wanted to make the most of this time. He needed to show her they could save their marriage.

"Is something wrong?" she asked.

The sight of the baby hooked up to beeping machines gave Jared second thoughts. His needs came a poor second to hers. "You want to take the first shift? I need to meet with Don."

Kate hung her jacket on the back of the chair, tidy as always. "That will be fine."

But it wasn't fine with Jared. He felt funny leaving them alone. His gaze returned to Cassidy.

"The baby will be fine, too." Kate's voice sounded a little strained.

He wasn't worried only about the baby. Kate looked so tired. Jared wondered if she'd eaten lunch. He would be gone for at least a couple of hours. What if she or Cassidy needed something?

"Go." Kate motioned to the door. "The sooner you're named personal representative, the sooner we get guardianship."

"If you need anything—"

"I'll call."

Would she? Kate, ever capable, never had called in the past. But he wouldn't stop hoping. "Please do."

He wondered if she heard him or if it mattered to her because she didn't look up as he walked to the door.

"Jared."

He turned.

"It's been a full day and—" she moistened her lips "—please be careful."

The concern in her voice brought a smile to his lips. Maybe she wasn't so indifferent to him after all. Maybe he stood a chance. "I'll be back, Kate. Just as soon as I can."

CHAPTER THREE

AN HOUR later, Kate struggled to keep her heavy eyelids open. A sleepless night and overloaded emotions had taken their toll on both her body and her brain, but she wasn't about to give into the exhaustion plaguing her. Not here in Cassidy's hospital room. What if the baby woke up, and Kate didn't hear her?

Sure, nurses came in and out with regularity, but she didn't want to let Susan down. Or, Kate realized, Jared.

All she needed was a second wind. Stretching her arms over her head, she wiggled her fingers. Caffeine would help, but she didn't want to leave Cassidy alone in case she woke up.

The minutes ticked by. Kate felt her head fall forward. Dazed and disoriented, she straightened. The smell screamed hospital and Kate knew where she was, but she still took in the cream-colored walls, the overhead lighting, a bed couch and a crib surrounded by noisy machines.

Cassidy.

The baby lay sound asleep. So small. So fragile.

And Kate's responsibility.

She sat with her back straight and the balls of her feet

pressed against the wall. Comfortable, no. But napping while on duty wasn't allowed.

Despite her brave words and determination, she was terrified of doing something wrong, of being unable to care for the baby the correct way. And the last thing Kate wanted was for Jared to find her asleep on the job. He held all the cards, or in this case, the baby. She wouldn't give him any reason to doubt her childrearing abilities.

From across the room, Kate stared at the crib. The machines lit and beeped, but the baby hadn't moved from her earlier position. Not since the nurse had been in here before. Cassidy hadn't made a sound, either. Unease prickled the hair at the back of Kate's neck.

Check her.

She imagined Susan's voice saying the words, and a heaviness weighed down on Kate. She'd lived with fear and uncertainty her entire childhood, and she'd moved beyond the two since becoming an adult. She'd put the past behind her, set goals and achieved them. But now Kate felt as if she'd been tossed into a whirlpool of doubt and confusion. She hated feeling that way again, and the million what-ifs running through her mind paralyzed her.

Kate remembered Susan telling her about checking the baby during the middle of the night to make sure Cassidy was breathing. Kate knew Susan's fears were irrational and told her to take advantage of the free time and sleep herself. Susan had smiled, but said nothing. Now Kate understood the new mother's anxiety. And she didn't like it one bit.

She shifted in her chair, uncomfortable with her new needy, uncertain self.

Where was Jared? Shouldn't he be back by now?

Kate glanced at the clock.

Darn. He'd only been gone an hour and with the paper-work that needed to be submitted to the court he wouldn't return anytime soon. She blew out a puff of air.

Jared.

Even if they disagreed most of the time, his presence here would comfort her, distract her. Especially if he gave her one of his dimpled smiles, the kind that spread all the way to his eyes. She hadn't seen one of those…in months. Not that she'd seen him, either.

A light blinked. Kate scanned the bank of machines. Surely if something was wrong, a monitor would sound an alarm and alert the nurse who would come running. She took a slow, deep breath.

Was this how her life would be from now on? Worried something bad would happen? Worried she would somehow fail Cassidy? Worried she would let Susan down in the worst possible way? If only Jared…

Kate shuddered. She had to stop. Now.

She didn't need Jared. She'd survived all but five years of her life without him. He'd proven he wouldn't stick around forever, that if she didn't do what he wanted he would leave. The realization provided resolve and courage, both of which she needed.

She could handle this. On her own. The way she'd always done.

All Kate needed to do was check the baby. She slipped off her shoes, walked softly to the crib and peered down. The rise and fall of Cassidy's chest brought a rush of relief. The sight of the slumbering child with a peaceful expres-sion on her face blanketed Kate with warmth. How could something so small make her feel so good? She fought the urge to caress the baby's smooth cheek. The last thing she wanted to do was wake the sleeping infant.

Kate stood by the crib. Watching the machines, with all those blinks and blips, would keep her busy until Jared returned. And then it would be his turn.

But she realized with unexpected clarity, her turn wouldn't be over. Not ever again. Her life would never be the same. Cassidy would always be a part of her life and link Kate to Jared. Even after the divorce...

The implications, both past and future, swirled through her mind. There would be no tidy goodbye. No tucking the memories away and forgetting about him. No moving on without Jared a part of her life. They would spend the next eighteen years making decisions about Cassidy, a child who would rely upon them for everything—nourishment, shelter, nurturing, advice and love.

The reality of what their new responsibility entailed hit Kate full force. She stood frozen, assailed by a multitude of doubt. She and Jared couldn't agree on what television show to watch or what they wanted for dinner on the weekends they were home together, how could they agree on what to do with Cassidy? Until she became an adult?

Kate staggered back.

What on earth had Susan been thinking?

Raising a child was nothing like baby-sitting Jared's nieces and nephews. Kate had no idea how to be a...mom. Motherhood had been this ideal, never anything real or attainable, just something she'd tucked away in the back of her mind when she realized her days as a wife were numbered. She didn't have a clue about being a parent. The only thing she knew was what kind of mother she didn't want to be.

And what about Jared? He had no experience being a dad. Sure, he liked kids, but that was different from having one of your own. With his travel schedule and once they were divorced…

Staring at the baby, Kate leaned against a wall. She didn't want to let her best friend down, but…

How in the world were she and Jared going to do this?

"How are you going to do this?" Not even a bad phone connection could mask the concern in Margery Reed's voice.

Jared wanted to reassure his mother, but no words would come. Not when he was as unsure about this situation as the rest of his family—two of whom he could hear voicing their opinions in the background.

"Raising a child isn't easy under the best of circumstances," Margery continued.

She meant his marriage. Or rather, his soon-to-be lack of one. The divorce had not only caught Jared off guard, but the entire Reed clan who had encouraged him to accept the promotion and move to Seattle with the belief Kate would follow him. Jared had assumed the same, that he was more important than her career. He'd assumed wrong.

"Being a single parent is going to be hard on Kate."

"Don't worry, Mom." Especially since he was the one who would end up with Cassidy, but he wasn't about to drop that bombshell on them yet. "We'll figure something out. Reeds always come out on top."

"You sound like your father."

"And Grandpa." A flashing sign caught Jared's attention. The Burger Barn. It was dinnertime. He doubted

Kate had eaten. She needed to put some weight back on. He pulled into the parking lot and lined up behind a red pickup truck in the drive-thru line. "You remember what Grandpa said. Second place is for everyone else."

Margery laughed. "You'll be saying the same thing to Cassidy before you know it."

An invisible weight pressed down on Jared. He had a good job and made recommendations to clients who would invest millions of dollars in companies based on his word, but that kind of responsibility was different than the parental kind. "Yeah. I guess I will."

"Chin up, Jared," Margery ordered. "You'll be a great dad."

Brady had written the same thing in his letter. Jared would do his best.

"I can't wait to meet Cassidy, our newest granddaughter."

He imagined her bragging to her friends about the newest addition to the family. If only it could have been under happier circumstances.

"Would you like us to come to Boise to help you?" his mom asked. "We could be there tomorrow. Tonight if you need us."

Yes. Please. He'd like nothing better than to dump this mess in his mother's experienced lap. But Jared swallowed the words before they were barely formed. He was in this on his own. Or rather, he was in this with Kate.

Once his family swarmed in on them, they would lose any chance of seeing if they could make this parenting thing work. He would lose any chance of showing Kate what she'd given up on. What they were both missing. What they could still have if only she wasn't so damn stubborn.

Okay, maybe that was nothing more than a pipe dream, but he wasn't ready to accept the failure of his marriage completely. Lawyers and divorce settlement aside.

Kate had never been comfortable accepting his parents' well-intentioned advice and assistance. She reminded him of a stray cat they'd found living in their garage when he was a kid. The cat wanted to be petted, but would hiss and arch if it received too much attention.

Jared knew his parents acted out of love, but the Reeds were like the cavalry when they rode into town with a cloud of dust in their wake. It was better to stand back and get out of the way to keep from being trampled. Kate would feel pushed out more than she already did if his family were here. For once Jared was willing to concede that point.

Cassidy was his and Kate's responsibility.

"Thanks, Mom, but let's see how we do on our own first."

"We? As in you and Kate?"

"The two of us were named guardians."

"But the divorce—"

"Isn't final yet," he interrupted. "And Cassidy needs both of us."

"Do you think...?" His mother's words trailed off.

"What?"

"It's none of my business."

That had never stopped her before. "What do you want to know, Mom?"

"Do you think that now with Cassidy in the picture, Kate will change her mind about the divorce?"

"I hope so," Jared admitted. "That would be the best thing for Cassidy."

"Would it be the best thing for you?" Margery pressed.

"Yes." Jared didn't hesitate with his answer. He wanted to avoid divorce at all costs.

"You know we love Kate, but be careful," his mother said. "We don't want to see you hurt again."

The red truck pulled forward. "I've got to go, Mom. I'll call you later."

"We'll be here. Love you."

Jared disconnected the call. He had no doubt his entire family would offer their advice and help. That was what the Reeds did.

You have your family to support you.

He remembered Brady's letter. Jared did have his family's support. And he might need it more than he ever had.

Time to stop wanting to get Kate back and do something about it. Jared would be taking a chance by putting their marriage—himself—on the line. Hell, she could say no and he would be worse off, but she could say yes and that was worth the risks. Because if she agreed…

Jared smiled. He would not only get his wife back. He would have the family he'd always dreamed about.

The smell of grease wafted in the sterile air of Cassidy's hospital room. Kate's stomach growled, and her mouth watered.

This wasn't good. Tired, hungry and hallucinating about food. Maybe she could ask one of the nurses for some crackers.

"How is Cassidy?"

The sound of Jared's softly spoken question brought a smile to Kate's face. She turned, and tingles shot through her at the sight of him. Okay, maybe seeing the bag of takeout and the drink holder with two large cups in his hands caused the tingling.

Whatever his other faults, Jared made sure she ate.

"She's doing well," Kate said. "She was awake for a little bit."

"Shouldn't we whisper so we don't wake her up?" he asked.

"The nurse said noise wouldn't bother her. If we're too quiet the baby will need total silence to sleep. The nurse recommended keeping music on in the house once we get home."

Wherever home might be. Portland, Kate hoped, until the divorce was final.

"That makes sense." Jared placed the bag on a table. "I brought double cheeseburgers, mustard and pickles only on yours, fries and onion rings."

Her empty stomach cheered. "My favorites."

A beat passed. "I remember."

And so did Kate. Grabbing lunch at a local burger joint and heading to the park for an impromptu picnic lunch on the rare occasion when they both happened to be in town on the same day, and it wasn't raining. She remembered eating and lounging on a blanket until the ringing of their cell phones told them it was time to return to work.

"Thanks." She offered him a smile. "I needed this."

But mere words didn't seem enough. Kate might not need Jared to be here, but she was happy he was here. She would have to do something nice for him.

"Thank you for staying with Cassidy," Jared said.

He handed her food and a drink. Kate wanted to gobble her dinner down, but she wasn't about to let hunger replace good manners. She would wait until Jared was ready.

He stood by the crib. "Go ahead and eat."

"I can wait." Kate sipped her soda instead. The jolt from the sugar and caffeine was exactly what she needed.

Jared's watchful gaze, however, made her uncomfortable. "What?" she asked.

He glanced back to the crib. "Let's eat before the baby wakes up."

She wasn't going to disagree.

Jared pulled his dinner from the bag, unwrapped his cheeseburger and took a bite. He wiped his mouth with a napkin. "I don't know about you, but I was starving."

Kate picked up a fry. "This hits the spot. I owe you."

"It's on me."

She hadn't meant owing him financially, but she understood his response. They had kept their own bank accounts after they married. Every month they would each deposit an equal amount into a joint household account to cover the mortgage payment and utility bills. The method worked well and made splitting the assets for the divorce settlement easy. "Thank you."

"You're welcome."

They finished eating in comfortable silence, a difference from the negative undercurrents they usually encountered when they were together.

Kate finished her soda and wiped her hands. "The nurse said the doctor might release Cassidy in two days, three at the most. Did you and Don finish going through the paperwork?"

"Completed and filed." Jared said to her relief. "Don hopes the court will appoint me personal guardian tomorrow so we can start the guardianship proceedings."

"And then the real fun begins."

"I've been thinking about this whole guardianship issue," Jared said.

"Me, too." Kate leaned back in the chair. "It isn't going to be easy. We don't know anything about babies."

"You're right, and this is going to be hard on Cassidy. She doesn't know what's going on or where her parents went so we need to make sure she's the priority."

"I agree," Kate said. "We need to think about Cassidy and the effect on her with every decision we make."

Suddenly the situation didn't seem so overwhelming to Kate. She wasn't alone. She and Jared were discussing matters logically, rationally, without disagreeing. A positive sign. She only hoped their getting along continued in the future.

Jared's easy smile sent Kate's heart beating faster. "Sounds like a good plan."

No doubt he felt the same way about their conversation and getting along. That bolstered her spirits and gave her the courage to ask what had been on her mind all afternoon. "Once Cassidy is released from the hospital, could I please take her back to Portland with me? At least until the divorce is final."

"Another good idea." He glanced at the crib, then back at Kate. "My family can watch Cassidy when you are at work. Unless you had thought of other arrangements?"

Child care. Kate hadn't thought about that, but a nanny or day care didn't make sense when the Reed clan was right there. And Susan wanted Cassidy to be part of a large family.

"I hadn't thought of any child care arrangements," Kate admitted. "Do you think your family will mind?"

He laughed. "They'll be fighting over her."

"That will be good for both Cassidy and me." And Susan. That was what she wanted. She must be smiling up in Heaven.

Except, Kate wondered, would she see the recrimination in Jared's family's eyes? Sure, they still invited her to dinner and gatherings, but she knew they weren't happy about the situation between her and Jared.

"I could come down and help out on weekends," he added.

"That would be great."

"Yeah, great."

His gaze locked with hers. The temperature in the room increased. She needed another soda or a glass of water or a…kiss. Kate looked down.

No, this couldn't be happening. Her reaction was simply due to the situation. The grief following the death of Susan and Brady. The emotion of inheriting Cassidy.

Kate wouldn't let herself think otherwise. "What about after the divorce?"

"I've been thinking about that," he said. "The best thing for Cassidy would be if she had a mother and a father who were married."

"I know that's what Susan and Brady would have preferred." Kate would give Jared that. "But in our case a traditional family is not possible."

A beat passed. "It is if we didn't get a divorce."

His words hung on the air.

Not divorce. That was the craziest idea she'd ever heard. Kate almost laughed except he wasn't smiling. The seriousness in his eyes told her he wasn't kidding. Okay, she could appreciate him making a noble suggestion for the baby's sake, but one of them had to be realistic.

"What difference would not divorcing make?" Kate asked. "We hardly saw each other when we lived in the same house. Now we live in different states. Staying married would never work."

"Don't you want Cassidy?" he asked.

That wasn't fair.

"You know I do." Kate wanted the baby with a fierceness that surprised her. "But staying married under our current circumstances—"

"Let's change the circumstances."

Hope squeezed her chest. Would he move back to Portland?

"What do you suggest?" she challenged, eager to hear his answer.

"I just…" He seemed at a loss for words. "Maybe things could be different between us."

Not good enough.

Kate wasn't about to allow Jared back into her life, into her bed, into her heart only to watch him leave and hurt her again. Unless…

She thought about her wedding rings locked away in a safe-deposit box at her bank. Losing weight had given her an excuse to take them off. She never thought she would put the gold band and diamond solitaire back on her finger. Her heart pounded.

"Things would have to be very different," she said, formulating the plan in her head.

It could work or cause even more problems. She gulped.

Jared eyed her warily. "What do you have in mind?"

Kate couldn't believe she was considering this, but she had no other choice if she wanted to keep Cassidy. And that was what she wanted. More than anything. She rubbed her thumb over her bare ring finger. "A marriage of convenience."

His brows furrowed. "A what?"

"A marriage in name only for Cassidy's sake."

A nerve throbbed on Jared's neck. "You'd go for that kind of marriage?"

She inhaled sharply. Logically she knew that kind of marriage would work. Emotionally... No, she wasn't going there.

"I would." This was the best solution for everyone involved. "How about you? Would you agree to a marriage of convenience?"

CHAPTER FOUR

"JARED?" Kate asked.

All he had to do was say yes, but a marriage of convenience wasn't what he had in mind.

She bit her lip, a nervous habit she'd had since they first met. "So what do you think?"

That she was out of her mind.

At least insanity would explain her "in name only" proposition. He would rather think her crazy than accept she was rejecting him all over again. When Kate said she wasn't moving to Seattle with him, he'd been upset. When she said she wanted a divorce, he'd been devastated. And now this...

His jaw clenched. He just didn't get her.

This morning, drawn together in grief, he'd felt closer to Kate than he had in months. But now he saw that she didn't want the same thing he did. That she didn't want to save their marriage the way he did.

The realization made his decision all the more critical. With differing expectations, this solution of hers could turn into a disaster and drive them further apart. That was the last thing he wanted. Especially with a baby involved.

"How would this work?" he asked.

"One of us would keep Cassidy during the week. Most likely me since your family could take care of her during the day," she explained, expounding on her plan with enthusiasm. Kate was always a great one for planning. "We could spend weekends together so people won't think we are separated."

Being separated, like divorced, would give him custody per the conditions of the will. Jared weighed the options. Okay, he could work with weekends. As long as she wasn't serious about this "in name only" stuff.

"We could alternate between Portland and Seattle," she continued. As she stared at Cassidy, the tenderness of Kate's gaze reminded Jared of how she used to look at him, and something twisted inside him. "Drive up on Fridays, come back on Sundays."

Weekdays apart, weekends together. That was more than she had been willing to do before. Some of his unease disappeared.

Sure, a long distance marriage wasn't what he wanted. Jared wanted Kate in Seattle full-time, but this was a step in the right direction. With the attraction buzzing like static between them, physical chemistry would soon take over. Kate would realize they belonged together and make the move north.

Now that would be a very convenient marriage. And worth whatever challenges and commute the next few weeks and months held. *If* things worked out the way he hoped they would.

"So…you, me and Cassidy will be together on the weekends," he stipulated.

"Well—" she wet her lips "—mostly together. We

would share the same house. You and I would still be legally married. We just wouldn't do some things other married couples do."

Uh-oh, but he'd heard the words "legally married," not divorced. Key point.

"So you'd continue to keep your name," he said, making sure he understood the intricacies. "We'd keep our finances separate. We'd live apart except on weekends."

That was how they lived now. And had before the separation. It had worked well for them then.

She scuffed the toe of her shoe against the floor. "It also means we won't be, um…"

"What?" he asked.

"Romantic."

She was serious. He smiled, hoping to tease her out of that position. "With a baby around, that's a given."

For now.

If they stayed in Portland over the weekend, his family could watch Cassidy so he and Kate could spend time alone and perhaps rekindle the romance.

"It's not just romance," she clarified. "It's also, you know…"

He was afraid he did know, but Jared wanted her to spell out the rules in case he was wrong. "I don't know."

"Sex."

"What about sex?" he asked.

"There won't be any."

There hadn't been any sex for a while. He didn't like that, but assumed once they were back together…maybe not right away, but eventually. "No sex for how long?"

She bit her lip again.

"Kate?"

"Never," she mumbled.

Not good. "Ever?"

She blushed. "Correct."

"But we're married."

"We'll stay married for Cassidy, not each other," Kate explained, as if she were ordering a cup of coffee not talking about their future together. "That's why it's called a marriage of convenience."

"That's totally inconvenient."

Stupid really.

No sane person would agree to something like that.

She shrugged.

"Let me get this straight." Jared imagined living in the same house with Kate and not touching her. Impossible. "There's no fooling around?"

"No."

"What about kissing?"

"I—I'm pretty sure kissing goes against the rules of an 'in name only marriage.'"

Screw the rules.

That wasn't a marriage. That was hell. Sure, he was managing the celibacy imposed by their separation, but he didn't want to live like that forever. With his own wife. "You really think we can live by those rules?"

"We can if we have to." She leaned forward and touched his arm. "For Cassidy's sake."

No way. Kate was too passionate to spend her life in a sexless marriage. Sure, she might think she could for Cassidy's sake and Kate might hold out a short while, but she wanted him as much as he wanted her. He'd bet money on it. She still had her hand on him.

And that, Jared realized, would work completely in his

favor. Plus it gave him an idea. A way to rattle Kate's neat little world and bring her back where she belonged.

"I've got to be honest with you, Kate," he said. "I don't think I can live like that."

She lowered her hand and her gaze. "I know it's a lot to ask to put aside all your own, um, needs and focus on the baby's. But don't all parents have to do that to some extent?"

I hope you and Kate have worked things out.

Brady's letter rushed back. He wanted his daughter raised by a married couple. And Jared wanted his wife back. He hated the idea of a divorce more than a sexless marriage, but if his idea worked, neither of those things would be a future concern. "What about other people?"

Her eyes widened. "What?"

Aha. That definitely got her attention. "What if we saw other people, discreetly of course, so long as our actions don't affect Cassidy?"

"I—I hadn't thought about that."

From her arched eyebrows, she didn't seem to like the idea, either. Good.

"I don't mean right away," he added smoothly, as if he'd given this a lot of thought, not coming up with the game plan as he spoke. "Maybe we could discuss this in say, six months. Once Cassidy is settled and we're more comfortable with the arrangement. I mean, marriage."

"So you're actually considering this?" Kate asked.

He was. He must be out of his mind, too. "Seeing other people?"

"No, the marriage of convenience."

Mentally he counted backward from ten.

"Yes." He forced himself not to smile at the surprise in

her eyes. Keeping the opponent guessing was the way to go if he wanted to win. And he wasn't about to lose. "But this no-sex thing is pretty much a deal breaker for me."

"Have you been seeing other people?"

Jackpot. He had her right where he wanted her. Curious about his social life without her. "No. I didn't think that was a good idea until the divorce was final."

"Oh."

He thought he glimpsed relief in her eyes. "What about you?"

"Me? No." Her cheeks reddened. "I mean, with work and everything, I never thought much about dating."

But she would now.

And that, too, would work entirely in his favor. Kate would never assume she was the only woman he wanted in his bed. "So what do you say?"

A beat passed. "O-kay."

He released the breath he'd been holding. "Okay?"

"The marriage is a legal one, not an emotional one." Her words didn't give him a warm and fuzzy feeling, but hey, it was better than a divorce. "I'm willing to consider this, um, seeing other people once we have the situation under control."

"Good." Because the discussion was never going to have to come up. Soon Jared would have Kate right where he wanted her. He would have what he wanted—his wife in Seattle with him, back in his life and back in his bed. Someday they would share a good laugh over all of this. "This is what's best for Cassidy."

And, Jared realized, it was the only way for him and Kate to save their marriage.

* * *

Later that night, Kate stood on the balcony of her hotel room. The crescent moon look painted on the star-filled black sky. A cool breeze ruffled her nightshirt, and she ignored the goose bumps on her arms and legs. She should be in bed, sleeping while she had the chance. But every time she closed her eyes a million thoughts took over her mind.

What had she done?

The sound of the rushing water from the river below matched the turmoil inside Kate. She clutched the wrought-iron railing.

She had never expected Jared to suggest they not divorce. Yes, he'd claimed he wanted to work things out, but his actions showed Kate he only wanted her in Seattle with him. That wasn't working things out. That was Jared winning his argument. Getting his way again.

But now…

They wouldn't be divorcing. They really wouldn't be married, either.

No sex.

She tucked her hair behind her ears. That would be…interesting. Impossible.

No, Kate amended, not impossible. If they kept their distance and locked their bedroom doors at night.

Correction, if she did that.

Jared seemed to have no problem agreeing to the rules so long as he could see other people discreetly. His request made sense. Sex had always been important to him. Obviously his feelings for her had changed. Her feelings had changed, too.

Still it wouldn't be easy. Boundaries would need to be set and adhered to. The love may have died between them, but the physical chemistry hadn't. Every time they touched, the pull of attraction drew them closer. And that meant she would have to keep her distance.

Or find someone else.

The idea left her feeling unsettled, sad even. Kate took a deep breath.

This whole situation was so unbelievable. What she needed was someone to talk to. Kate glanced into the room and saw her cell phone sitting on the bed, but the one person she could call, the one person she could count on to help her was no longer here to answer the telephone.

Susan.

The thought of her dead friend brought a wave of grief. The jumble of emotions—sorrow, confusion, frustration—brought tears to Kate's eyes, but she wasn't about to cry again. Not even in the solitude of her hotel room, in the inky darkness of the late night sky. This was a time for strength. No matter how weak she might feel.

Cassidy. Kate had to think about Cassidy and what Susan had wanted for her:

> She can have what we didn't have growing up. I need that for my child. Grandparents, aunts, uncles, a ton of cousins. Do you understand? I want you to understand this, Kate, and support it. I need you to be a part of Cassidy's life no matter what has happened with you and Jared.

And Kate would.

Knowing she was making Susan's dream for her daughter come true, Kate could do anything. Even spend the next eighteen years being married to Jared Reed.

Cassidy would have both a mother and a father who

loved her. The pattern of Susan's and Kate's childhood would not be repeated. She prided herself on her control and the ability to do what needed to be done. Those skills would never be more important, when Cassidy's well-being and future depended on Kate's action. She would push aside her emotions. She would live knowing Jared would be her husband, but he would never really be hers again. She would make practical, meaningful decisions for herself and Cassidy.

Kate would become the perfect mother.

Because, she realized, that's all she could do.

The next morning at the hospital, Kate juggled a drink holder and a bag from Starbucks. The aroma of freshly brewed house blend coffee made her crave a sip. After another restless night, caffeine would definitely help, but first she wanted to see Jared. No, Cassidy. Kate was here for the baby.

She pushed open the door to the room with her shoulder, took a step inside and froze.

Both Jared and Cassidy were still sound asleep. Part of Kate—the sleepy part—was envious, and the other part—mainly her overwhelmed emotions—found the scene in front of her totally heartwarming. Jared slept on the sofa bed with an arm outstretched toward Cassidy. Kate wondered if he'd fallen sleep touching the baby. Her heart constricted at the sweet image.

In that moment, she could almost believe Cassidy would solve all their problems and make them the perfect couple they'd once been. But a few seconds of daydreaming was all Kate could allow herself because she knew better.

Not even the adorable Cassidy could bridge the gap of

problems that had pushed Kate and Jared apart. Children, and when to have them, had been only one of their problems. Jared hadn't wanted to wait any longer to start a family. He hadn't cared about Kate's company or her employees or her dreams. He'd wanted her pregnant and in Seattle. With him.

No compromise. No discussion.

Sure he suggested marriage counseling, but only to a therapist who was a friend of the Reeds and would take his side. The way his family had.

Misgivings over this marriage of convenience exploded in Kate. Her heart beat triple time. Their differences—what they wanted from their lives, their career, pretty much everything—wouldn't just go away. Divorce or not.

Panic threatened to overwhelm her. Kate placed the bag and drinks on the bed table. She wanted to tell Jared she wanted out. Removing the plates, she looked at him and the baby.

Her best friend's beautiful baby girl.

Kate's heart rate slowed. She couldn't forget she was doing this for Cassidy. Susan and Brady, too. In control, Kate pulled out the fresh fruit bowls, pastries, forks and napkins.

Jared stirred in the sofa bed. As he stretched his arms over his head, his gaze zeroed in on Cassidy. He turned Kate's way. "You brought coffee and a continental breakfast buffet."

Ignoring his charming smile, Kate picked up a scone. "I thought you might be hungry."

"Thanks." Jared stood, his shirt wrinkled and his pants creased. He looked sleep rumpled and adorable, reminding her of the times he'd come straight home after a long flight and tumbled into bed with her. Sleep the last thing on either of their minds. Heat emanated deep within her.

"Is something wrong?" he asked, grabbing a pastry.

No sex. No fooling around. No kissing. Seeing other people discreetly.

"Why do you think anything's wrong?" she asked.

"Well, you lost your best friend, gained a child and you have that tongue between your teeth look you get when something's on your mind."

She didn't know what to make of his observation. "There is a lot on my mind." But she wasn't about to admit thinking about making love to him was one of them. "That's how it's going to be for a while."

"A long while I'd imagine." He sipped his coffee. "This hits the spot. You went above and beyond as usual."

As usual. She ate her scone. It felt weird to be having breakfast with him like this. To remember how life had been between them and how different life would be from now on. Kate wasn't sure how to act or what to do, but she guessed pushing the hair that had fallen across his forehead back into place wouldn't be a good idea.

"Did you sleep?" Jared asked.

"Some." Kate would guess four, maybe five hours. After exhaustion had extinguished the thoughts in her head. "How about you?"

"I slept pretty well." He rubbed his neck. "Though the sofa bed was about as comfortable as a seat in coach on a trans-Pacific flight."

Kate glanced at Cassidy. "How did the baby do?"

"She fussed a bit." He walked over to the crib. "It took a while to get her to take a bottle."

"You fed her?" Kate asked.

"I did." His mouth quirked in a lopsided smile. "I got to hold her, too."

No fair. Her skin prickled. "The nurse wouldn't let me do that."

Laughter glimmered in his eyes. "You must not have the right touch."

He was only kidding, but his words stabbed Kate's heart like a dozen daggers. She'd wanted to hold Cassidy and feed her, too, but the nurse had said no. Kate hadn't taken it personally. Until now.

Stricken, she looked at him.

"They finally disconnected the machines," he explained. "That's the reason I got to hold her."

Kate felt foolish. She had to stop with all the insecurities plaguing her. She had more important things to worry about. "That means Cassidy is improving. And if she's released early…"

"I'm meeting with Don this morning to talk about the guardianship." Jared's tone brought reassurance. "Don't worry, Kate. This is all going to work out. I promise you."

He'd promised to love her, in good times and in bad. That had only lasted three years. Cassidy needed them for the long haul. A shadow of doubt crossed Kate's heart.

"We have to make this work," she said.

"We will."

She wanted to believe him, but leaving their problems—and the emotions associated with them—in the past wasn't so easy. Kate wasn't sure she wanted to try. All they needed to do was be civil to each other on weekends. Anything more was asking for trouble.

She removed her jacket. "I guess you'll be off now."

He took a sip of coffee. "I don't mind staying a while."

But she minded.

Yes, they would have to work together for Cassidy's sake, but Kate wanted—no, needed—some space. The way he looked, the words he said, the response her body had to him. She was too upset to think clearly. She would be better off alone with Cassidy and get used to how life would be once they got home.

"Don't you have to meet Don?" Kate asked.

"Yes, but I have time." Jared's gaze returned to the baby. "Cassidy needs her family with her."

Family.

The word made Kate's head swim. She sat in the chair. Her entire life she'd dreamed of being part of a family. Sometimes she had been until fate or the state of Oregon interfered. She was a member of the Reed clan by marriage. But now with Cassidy and Jared, the three of them would be their own family, too.

The baby screeched. The sound, more pterodactyl than human, pierced the silence of the room. Kate jerked to her feet, and Jared hurried to the crib. He picked the baby up as if he'd been doing this all his life, not random nights when they baby-sat. The crying continued. He rocked Cassidy in his arms and then...silence.

Kate stared in amazement.

"Good morning, princess," Jared said. He cuddled Cassidy close, and Kate's heart lurched. "Did you have sweet dreams?"

Her mouth went dry. Unlike other women she knew, she'd never felt the ticking clock. She'd never experienced the overwhelming desire to have a baby. But seeing Jared with Cassidy in his arms sent Kate's world spinning off its axis. He'd always said he wanted children, and for the first time she could see he was meant to be a dad. An incredibly sexy, desirable dad. She couldn't tear her gaze away.

"Want a turn?" he asked.

She wanted…him.

No, Kate corrected, she wanted to hold the baby. "Please."

She cradled the warm, wiggly girl against her. She made sure to support the baby's head and neck the way she'd read online last night. Cassidy made a sucking motion with her mouth.

"She likes you," he said.

"She's hungry." But that was enough for the time being.

Kate touched her finger to the baby's tiny hand. Little fingers wrapped around hers. An instinctive reaction? Kate didn't care. All she knew was she could get used to this.

And that scared her.

She'd lost everyone she'd come to love. How would this be any different? "You can take her."

Jared placed his hands on her shoulders. "It's going to all work out, Katie."

She wanted to believe him. Desperately.

Staying married to Jared was the best thing for the baby, Kate knew that in her heart, but with his touch burning through the fabric of her blouse and his warm breath heating the blood in her veins, Kate wished she knew if this marriage was the best thing for her, too.

Because she wasn't sure.

She wasn't sure of anything.

CHAPTER FIVE

As JARED sat behind the wheel of the idling rental car two days later, the reality of what he'd inherited slammed into him. He gripped the gearshift. Forget speeding around town in his fully restored 1966, cherry-condition Corvette. He needed a new car, a family car, maybe that minivan he'd imagined. But that wasn't all he needed.

He glanced at Kate in the passenger seat. Her whole package sure had come together nicely today with her black pants, blue shirt, crystal jewelry and shoes. The only thing missing—her wedding rings.

"Are you ready?" he asked.

Cassidy squealed before Kate could answer.

Using the rearview mirror, he saw the back of the car seat. At least the most important passenger was ready to leave the hospital. The little cutie.

"Do you think the baby is strapped in tight enough?" Kate asked.

"Yes. She's not going anywhere." Jared thought about the accident, about Cassidy in that same model of car seat and surviving the horrific crash that claimed the lives of her parents. There'd been no doubt in Jared's mind which car seat to buy when he'd gone to the store yesterday. He would make sure nothing happened to Cassidy. "I stopped by the fire station and they double-checked the car seat installation and the nurse made sure Cassidy was securely strapped in."

Kate glanced back. "I wish we could see her face."

"The car seat has to face backward until she's one year old," he explained. "We can buy a mirror to see her face tomorrow."

"Maybe I should ride back there with her until then."

"Is that what Susan did?" he asked.

"No, but maybe if she had…"

Jared's heart hurt for Kate, but what-ifs would only make the grief process harder. With all the work getting the estates in order, there hadn't been much time to think about Susan and Brady. Maybe Jared and Kate needed to concentrate less on the To Do list and more on themselves, and each other. "Do whatever makes you comfortable, Katie."

The baby made popping noises with her mouth. At least Cassidy didn't seem to mind being in the car.

"Just drive," Kate said finally. "The baby seems happy."

That was good enough for him. He shifted the car into gear and released the brake. Kate sucked in a breath.

"Nervous?" he asked.

"No," she said. "Why would you think so?"

The tightness around her mouth was a dead giveaway, but he wasn't about to admit that to her. "We're on our own. No button to call the nurses' station if we need help. No one a few feet away to answer our questions. No one to pop into the room to give us a break."

"You sound like the nervous one."

Jared shrugged. "Life as we knew it has changed, but people deal with a new baby every day. We'll be fine."

"Yes, we will."

"Though I expected a little more than the nurse handing us the discharge papers, wishing us good luck and sending us on our way," he admitted. "Most people have nine months to prepare for parenthood. You think the hospital would have given us a manual or something."

"I know," she said. "Not much you can do with 'good luck.'"

That was more like the Kate he knew and loved.

Come back to me, baby.

"At least we have Susan's baby books," Kate continued. "I've been going through them."

"Good." He turned out of the hospital entrance and onto the road. "At least one of us will know what we're doing."

"You seem to have a pretty good handle on parenting." She glanced his way. "Cassidy likes you."

"She has excellent taste." If only Kate felt the same way about him. Patience. He had to give them time to work things out. "But all I did was hold her."

"And walk her and rock her and sing to her," Kate said. "The nurses gave me a full report."

Taking credit for doing what he needed to do in this case felt…wrong. He might be using the baby to get Kate back, but Cassidy's needs were the top priority. "It was the least I could do. The same as you."

Kate nodded. "We have a steep learning curve head of us. Vaccines, checkups, illnesses, diaper rash. I don't even want to think about trying to feed her solids. What if she's as picky as Brady?"

"Then we buy a side of beef and learn how to disguise vegetables as candy."

We. Not I. This was going to work. Jared tapped his thumb against the steering wheel. Soon Cassidy would soon have a mommy and daddy who lived together and loved each other, too.

"What?" Kate asked.

"You sound like a mom."

"Really?"

The hope contained in the one word surprised Jared. Kate always seemed so in control, so self-assured with everything, but her eager tone made her seem vulnerable and more…real. He liked that. "Yes, you sound like a mom."

A satisfied look settled on her face. "That's the nicest thing you've ever said to me."

"Interesting. Saying you sound like a mom works better than saying you look hot." He laughed. "I'll have to remember that."

"Trying to put a game plan into place if you need a night out with the boys?"

He smiled. "More like how to get out of the doghouse."

She smiled back. "Don't forget flowers and chocolate are good for that, too."

Yes. A point in his favor. Jared pumped his fist.

"Both hands on the wheel," Kate said.

"Sorry." He grabbed the steering wheel. "I won't forget."

He glanced at his rearview mirror. Flashing lights rapidly approached. A siren grew louder. Slowing down, he changed lanes. An ambulance roared past, its siren blaring.

The baby cried.

"She must not like sirens," Jared said.

"She doesn't like being woke up so suddenly or with so much noise." Kate reached back. "It's okay, Cassidy, we're here."

The baby wailed.

Kate sighed. "I should have sat in the back seat with her."

"Maybe she'll settle down."

"I can climb back there."

The image of Brady's mangled car flashed through Jared's mind. He didn't want Kate to unbuckle her seat belt. "We only have a few miles to go."

The crying worsened. No matter what either of them said, Cassidy wouldn't be consoled. Jared couldn't concentrate on the road. "Did you read anything in the baby books that would help calm her down?"

"No. She could be tired, hungry, wet... I don't know." Kate twisted in her seat. "We're going to be home soon, Cassidy. Do you miss your room? All your toys?"

The baby's cries squeezed Jared's heart. "I'm getting off the freeway at the next exit."

"We have to do something now."

"The radio," he offered.

"Noise is only going to upset her more." Frustration laced each of Kate's words. He knew exactly how she felt. The wailing reverberated around him.

"What do you suggest I do?" he asked.

When she didn't answer, Jared turned on the radio. A classical song played. Mozart, if he wasn't mistaken. The baby screeched. So much for those classical CDs he'd packed for her.

Jared hit one of the radio's preset buttons. A country music singer sang of lost loves and dented fenders. More crying. He pressed another button. A rock and roll tune filled the car with an electric guitar solo. Cassidy shrieked.

Tension in the car ratcheted. Kate grimaced. "This isn't working."

The baby hiccupped between her sobs.

Jared wasn't about to give up. He hit the AM dial and searched the stations, stopping when he heard stock quotes. Brady used to listen to this.

"Why are you putting on this station?" Kate reached for the radio. "It's only going to—"

Cassidy stopped crying as if someone had flicked an off switch.

"No way." Kate's arm hovered in front of the radio for a moment before she placed her hand on her seat. "How did you know financial news would work?"

"Brady listened to this station."

As a reporter spoke about an upcoming meeting to discuss interest rates, the baby squealed, a happy noise this time.

"We're going to have to add the money station in Portland to our presets," Kate said.

"It's already one of mine."

"Then maybe it's one of mine. I rarely listen to the radio."

"Too many phone calls."

"Yes, but I can maximize my productivity. That will be even more important now with Cassidy."

"I have no doubt you can do whatever you set your mind to." He wanted to reassure Kate. Hell, he wanted to take her in his arms and kiss some sense into her gorgeous head. "We both will do whatever it takes."

"You sound so sure."

"I am."

"Aren't you worried about the future?" she asked.

"All we can do is our best."

"What if that's not enough?" She leaned her head back against the seat. "I keep thinking about all these things."

"Like what?" Jared asked.

"I wonder what Cassidy will remember as she grows up. Will she remember Susan and Brady?"

"We will keep her memories alive," Jared said. "Even if she never remembers being born or living in Boise, we can tell her about that. We can tell her stories about Brady and Susan so Cassidy will always love them. And we can take her to Maine to meet her grandparents."

"It sounds like you've been thinking about this."

"Yes," he admitted. "Going through Brady and Susan's things has made it hard not to. I realized that's one reason they chose us. Who better to keep their memory alive in their daughter's life than their best friends?"

Kate nodded.

He caught a glimpse of affection in her eyes. Unexpected emotion rushed through him, and Jared struggled to maintain his composure.

"I've been setting aside the items I think we should keep for Cassidy, but there's probably stuff I haven't thought of," he said. "Guys aren't programmed to think that way."

"You're not like most guys, Jared Reed." Kate covered his hand with hers and squeezed. "Most guys wouldn't have done half of what you've done this week. And fewer would have thought about what things to save for a four-month-old baby."

As she pulled her hand away, Jared wished she could keep it there. Still her words gave him hope that one day soon they would put the past behind them and be a real family. The way Susan and Brady had wanted. The way Jared wanted. He only had to persuade Kate to want them to be a real family, too.

Sitting on the floor of Cassidy's nursery, Kate taped the lid of the box full of toys and board books. She glanced at Cassidy. The baby sat in her stroller, patting the activity bar with chubby fingers. The sight brought much needed comfort to Kate. After two days of sorting through items at Susan's house, a heavy sorrow had taken permanent residence in Kate's heart. She made a conscious effort to breathe.

"All done," she announced to Jared.

"Good timing," he said, looking as good in his sweats and T-shirt as he did in a suit and tie. "We have to leave for the airport in a few minutes. Though with this weather, the flight could be delayed."

Thunder and lightning had set an ominous mood this morning, and sheets of rain fell from the dark, gray skies. The constant pelting against the roof had worsened with each passing hour. The dreary weather fit Kate's mode better than the warm, sunny days they'd had all week. Finally the Heavens were mourning the loss of Susan and Brady, too.

But you would never know anything was wrong by Cassidy's cheery disposition. The baby looked so happy, so content, playing with the spinning toy in front of her. And why not? She was home, playing in the bedroom her parents had spent months decorating, lovingly painting pink and yellow stripes and stenciling flowers and butterflies. Cassidy might not notice the details, but the baby had to sense she was where she belonged.

Unfortunately she wouldn't be here much longer.

On Monday, the house would be put up for sale.

Poor Cassidy. She had no idea what was in store for her. A part of Kate didn't want to leave Boise, didn't want to take Cassidy away from the house Brady and Susan had called home.

"Hey." Jared tapped Kate's shoulder. "You okay?"

Not trusting her voice, she nodded.

"Leaving is going to be hard," he said, matching her own thoughts. "But we have to do it."

Kate nodded again. Selling the house made sense, but left her feeling guilty for taking the baby with her to Portland.

He carried the last box from the bedroom to the pile of stuff in the living room. Movers would transport everything to her home in Portland. The rest of the items would be sold or donated to charity.

Getting rid of a houseful of possessions seemed sad and wrong. She wished Susan and Brady were still alive and none of this had ever happened. If only… Kate hugged her knees.

The cloudy skies seemed to lighten. The rain stopped. Sunlight streamed into the room through the nursery's pair of double-hung windows. The rays, defined by the particles in the air, surrounded the stroller. Giggling, Cassidy reached toward the sunshine.

The baby, who had never seemed so animated before, mesmerized Kate.

"What do you think she sees?" Jared asked from the doorway.

"I don't know," Kate admitted. "Maybe she can feel the sun's warmth. Susan used to call it a sun kiss."

Kate wished she could reach out and grab hold of one of the rays, one of the sun kisses. Her house needed a dose of sunshine badly. So did she. Maybe Cassidy would bring some with her to Portland.

"Whatever the baby sees, she likes it," Jared said.

Cassidy's little arms wiggled in the air as if she wanted to be picked up but she wasn't looking at either Kate or Jared. And she wasn't crying.

"She's happy," Kate agreed. "That's what matters."

"You're right about that."

She took comfort in their ability to agree about the baby. The willingness to get along for Cassidy's sake would make things—okay, their future—easier.

"You've got a smudge of newsprint ink on your cheek." Jared wiped her face with his thumb. "There. All gone."

His nearness disturbed her. He smelled good, a mix of fresh soap and raw earth from his work in the yard. "Th-thanks."

His gaze captured hers. "You're welcome."

Kate expected him to remove his hand from hers. He didn't.

She waited. And waited.

Common sense told her to look away, but she didn't want to listen. Cassidy's coos and giggles told Kate the baby was fine so there was no need to look at her.

"I feel weird not going with you," Jared said.

"You have important business to finish up here."

"I know, but…"

The tone of his voice worried her. "What?"

He didn't answer.

She searched his face for a sign as to what he was thinking, feeling, but found nothing. "Jared?"

"It's going to be strange not having you—" he looked at the baby "—and Cassidy with me."

Cassidy. This was about the baby. Kate ignored the twinge of disappointment inching down her spine. She should be pleased he cared so much about the baby already. Maybe he wouldn't walk away again. What was she thinking? Jared might have left her, but he would never leave Cassidy. "You'll see her next weekend."

"And you."

What he said shouldn't affect Kate, but an unexpected lump formed in her throat. Jared had been a rock, supporting her during the moving funeral service and boxing up Susan and Brady's house. He'd kept things moving and her going. Suddenly a week apart seemed like forever.

"Kate…"

The way he said her name made her pulse quicken.

"I'm happy we had time together this week," he said.

Her temperature shot up.

His lips curved in a half smile. "I'm going to miss you."

Her mouth went dry.

Jared lowered his face toward hers, toward her lips.

He was going to kiss her.

Her heart slammed against her ribs.

Grief, loss, exhaustion. Those emotions explained the physical reactions she was having to him. That was all her body's responses were, all they could be.

She should step back, put distance between them. But Kate couldn't. She didn't want to move away.

"It's time we headed to the airport," he whispered and kissed her forehead.

Relief mingled with regret at the brush of his lips. A silly reaction, really. Good thing she and Cassidy were leaving.

Kate appreciated all Jared had done this week. She'd leaned on him, more than she ever had in the past, but she had to get used to being on her own again. A peck on the forehead, a tender glance and a sincere word changed nothing. She was the one who had to juggle her routine with the baby's. Kate had misgivings, but she could do it. She'd always done everything herself.

But the thought didn't cheer her up. After this week with Jared, it only made her feel a whole lot worse.

Back in Portland, the telephone rang. Grimacing, Kate ran from the pile of pink and pastel-colored laundry sitting on the couch to the receiver on the kitchen counter. She didn't want the ringing to wake Cassidy.

"Hello." Kate sounded rushed and frustrated. She didn't care. Chances were the caller had the wrong number or was a telemarketer. She'd had one of each tonight. Why would this be any different? People she knew called her cell phone. She should just turn off the ringer.

"Hello, Kate."

The sound of Jared's voice brought a rush of anxiety. He never called on the home number. "Is something wrong?"

"No, I wanted to see how you and Cassidy were doing."

"We're doing, um, okay." Kate tried to sound enthusiastic, but she felt like an absolute failure at motherhood. Talk about on-the-job training at its worst, and she only had Cassidy in the morning and after work. She felt a tremendous rush of relief and guilt each time she dropped Cassidy off at Jared's parents' house or picked her up at one of Jared's sisters' houses. Kate couldn't imagine being the full-time caretaker. Of course, the weekend was coming up. "We're adjusting."

Sort of.

"That's great," he said, sounding pleased.

"Yes, great." So long as she continually held Cassidy, only slept a few hours a night and totally let the house go. Kate adjusted the cordless receiver and folded a pink onesie. The amount of laundry one baby generated amazed her.

"My mom says Cassidy's grown."

Kate attributed the baby's weight gain on her own exhaustion. How much could a baby grow in less than a week? "She's still the same diaper size."

"My sister said she uses cloth diapers," Jared said. "Do you think we should use cloth diapers?"

"No." The word tumbled from Kate's mouth. She could barely keep up with the laundry now. "Brady and Susan used disposables. Let's not change anything more in Cassidy's life."

Or mine.

"That's a good point."

Thank goodness he agreed. Kate folded a burp cloth and made a mental note to buy more of them to protect her clothes.

"Do you need anything?"

You. Strike that.

She needed an extra six hours a day to catch up with work here at home and at the office. Despite all the books and magazine articles she'd read, combining work with motherhood required a tricky balance. One she wasn't close to mastering.

"No, thanks. I'm figuring things out." Or would. Getting used to having another person completely reliant upon her wasn't easy. She didn't know how other moms managed especially those without a husband to help. "Though I see the benefit of maternity leave now."

Kate had dreamed of a smooth transition, of how wonderful being a mother and working a fulfilling job would be. Reality crushed her expectations. Her life at home was a far cry from the perfect baby who slept at night and smiled all the time. At work, she finally understood the undercurrent of tension between the women in the office who had children and those who didn't.

Exhausted and completely unorganized for the first time in her life, she didn't know how to make things work when she barely had time to think. Kate folded a lavender sleeper.

"Do you think that would help?" Jared asked.

Oh, no. What was she going to say? "It, um, might."

"Is a leave of absence a possibility?"

"No. Not right now." A part of her felt guilty for not taking this week off to be with Cassidy, but she wasn't about to admit that to Jared. Since she owned the company, she wouldn't have to qualify for family leave. She could simply stay home, but that wouldn't be good for her clients or employees. "I shouldn't have brought it up."

"You sound tired."

Of course she did. Sleeping in three to four hour bursts drove a person to exhaustion. Ever since arriving in Portland Cassidy wouldn't sleep during the middle of the night. She wanted to be held and rocked or held and walked. So that was what Kate did, and she was feeling the effects. She'd fallen asleep at lunch today. "It's been a busy week."

"I know how that goes."

He might think so, but he didn't. Jared couldn't.

Once upon a time, before pink clothing, bottles of formula and wet diapers had become a way of life, Kate believed she'd known the definition of a busy week just like Jared.

She hadn't even been close.

Not until Cassidy. But Kate couldn't tell him that or he would think she couldn't cope.

"Where are you?" she asked.

"Raleigh, North Carolina."

"I thought you were going to Chicago."

"Change of plans," he said. "I'm flying to Portland on Friday, and I'll take the train to Seattle on Sunday night."

Kate glanced around the house. She'd yet to unpack the boxes from Boise. The clutter and mess embarrassed her. She wanted the house to look perfect when Jared arrived. "Do you need a ride from the airport?"

"I'll have my parents pick me up or I'll take a shuttle."

"I don't mind," she said.

"Don't worry about me."

"But I do worry." The words escaped before she could stop them. "I mean, not all the time. But sometimes."

She should shut up before she made a bigger fool of herself. Maybe she needed another nap. Or a good night's sleep.

"I worry about you sometimes, too," he said. "So that makes us even."

Somehow Kate couldn't ever see the scales between them being equal, but she appreciated the thought.

"I'd better get going," he said. "I have work to finish. I'll call you later."

"Only if you have time." She had stuff to do, too. Her list of things to check off by Friday kept growing by the minute.

"I'll make the time."

"For Cassidy," Kate said.

"And you," Jared said. "I miss both of my girls."

"Your girls miss you." Kate had missed him, more than she thought she would.

His rich laughter filled the phone. "Give Cassidy a kiss for me. And here's one for you."

Smack. With that, he hung up.

A burst of heat pulsed through Kate's veins. Too bad she couldn't get a real-honest-to-goodness-husband-to-wife-kiss—from him because that was what she really wanted.

Stop. She shouldn't be having those kinds of feelings about Jared.

She'd told him not to kiss her. She'd told him they would discuss seeing other people in six months. She'd told him their marriage would not be emotional. But, she realized, those were all the things she wanted from him.

Oh, no. Kate sunk to the ground. Now what was she going to do?

CHAPTER SIX

THE porch light wasn't on. The door was locked. And since Kate had filed for divorce, Jared no longer had a key. He grimaced and rang the doorbell.

A minute ticked by. And another.

Not good. He wasn't sure what to expect when he arrived home, but Jared's hope that Kate would be happy to see him plummeted. Standing out here in the dark, he feared she might have changed her mind about their arrangement. And if that happened... He jammed his finger on the doorbell again.

After another minute passed, he pulled out his cell phone, but before he could call her, the door opened.

She stood holding a flushed, crying Cassidy. "Sorry I took so long."

The sound of Kate's frustrated voice made him want to wrap his arms around her, but no matter how much he might want to embrace her, he couldn't. Not yet. They were still tiptoeing across a tightrope with no net below. One wrong move and they would go splat. "Looks like you have your hands full."

He wasn't kidding.

The stark-white bandage around Cassidy's little head, the tears streaming down her round cheeks and the "save me" look in Kate's eyes, reminded Jared he wasn't the only one adjusting to a new set of circumstances. He wanted to help make things better for all of them.

She shrugged. "I was upstairs rocking her, but that only irritated her more."

"Having a tough time, baby." Jared ran his finger along Cassidy's smooth cheek. She screamed. He jerked his hand away. "Is she okay?"

"Yes." Kate rocked back and forth, and Cassidy stuffed her fist in her mouth and sulked. "She doesn't like going to bed."

Jared didn't understand. She was a baby. His sister said babies slept a lot. "Maybe she's hungry."

"She just had a bottle."

"Could be gas," he offered.

"I burped her."

"Wet?" he asked.

"I just changed her."

"Does her head hurt?" His did, from the noise and hunger. If he were a baby, he'd probably cry, too.

Kate glared at him. "Are you suggesting I don't know enough to take care of her?"

"No." Hell, no. "You're taking great care of her."

"I'm trying." Kate's shoulders slumped. "But she wants to be held. All the time."

That explained the dark circles under Kate's eyes and why she looked a bit messy with stains on her purple silk blouse and spots on her brown pants. And he'd never seen her with her hair haphazardly piled on top of her head and clipped that way. Jared couldn't believe how much she'd let her "whole package" slip. Even with a crying baby in her arms.

Seeing Kate look so…untidy took a little getting used to, but the tousled style was cute on her.

He liked that she hadn't forgotten the most important piece of jewelry in her wardrobe. She wore her wedding set—a plain gold band and an engagement ring. The diamond sparkled as if newly cleaned. He wondered if she'd had it resized or started eating better.

Jared placed his luggage inside. Ready to be the go-to-guy, he closed and locked the door. But facing his two girls, he wasn't sure where to begin. Kate looked as if she needed a shoulder to cry on. Cassidy, all teary-eyed and slobbery, clung to Kate. Maybe he should remove his jacket with all this crying action going on. "I, uh, don't mind holding her."

Cassidy wailed. Jared gritted his teeth.

Kate turned her away from him. "I've got her."

Barely.

He wasn't sure he could do any better, but he owed it to both of them to try. "You do, but I'm here. Get some sleep."

"I'm fine."

But she wasn't. He could see the tiredness in her eyes and the strain on her face. The screaming baby was a pretty big clue, too. Kate, however, was being Kate and doing everything herself. He didn't want her handling child rearing the same way she handled everything else in her life.

"We're in this together," he said.

Not that he knew what he was going to do once he had Cassidy. Truthfully the idea of holding a fussy—okay, crying—baby appealed to him as much as a visit with the IRS about his tax return. Still he had to do something.

Kate gave no response. She simply swayed with the baby in her arms.

Tension simmered in the air. Cassidy fussed and flailed.

Usually when Kate acted like this, needing to do things her way, they'd go head to head then have hot makeup sex. Jared wouldn't mind the latter, but he wasn't sure that was the way to go this time. She didn't seem up for a disagreement, let alone a fight. The only thing she seemed up for was bedtime. He kind of liked it.

This new disheveled Kate was growing on him. She seemed less in control, more vulnerable and to be honest, sexier than her normally put-together, perfect, whole package self. Not that he would ever admit that to her.

The baby punched the air like a fighter warming up for the second round.

"Please." Jared extended his arms. "I want to hold her. I kinda missed her."

And you.

But he wasn't about to go there. Not yet.

Patience. He needed to tattoo the word on his brain so he wouldn't push her too hard and too fast.

"Are you sure?" she asked.

"Positive."

With only the slightest hesitation, Kate handed him the baby. As her hand brushed his during the transfer, he felt a shock. Electric static? Or physical attraction? Maybe a little of both. Jared didn't care. Having her soft skin against his skin, even if it had been for less than a nanosecond, felt good.

"Hello, sweet pea," he said to Cassidy.

A sob greeted him.

"Now is that any way to say hello to me?"

Another cry.

As Jared held the warm bundle close, the baby's scent surrounded him. Not all sugar and spice. And he missed the smell of Kate's grapefruit shampoo. Cassidy smelled different...funny. Formula? Or maybe that diaper needed changing again.

She wiggled. Sighed. And then her entire body seemed to go boneless. Magic. Relaxed didn't begin to describe how content she looked. Something inside of him melted. Jared smiled. "Have you been giving Kate a hard time?"

Kate pushed an errant strand of hair back into her clip. "Except for not sleeping, she's been great."

Cassidy reached her chubby little hands to touch his chin, but missed. "Ah-goo."

"Ah-goo?" Flattered, disarmed, he touched her nose. "Really?"

The baby grinned, all toothless gums and drool, and Jared knew he was a goner. Okay, maybe Kate had another reason for wanting to keep hold of Cassidy instead of control issues—baby love. "You are so cute."

Kate tsked. "You better be careful or she'll have you wrapped around her little finger."

Too late.

"Nothing wrong with that." As he rocked back and forth, Jared glanced into the living room. The house, as usual, reminded him of a model home with nothing out of place. Even the magazines on the coffee table were aligned perfectly. Not that he expected any less. Kate was a neat freak plus she had a housecleaner come every other week. Except something—boxes to be exact—were missing.

"Did the movers come?" he asked.

She nodded.

"Where is everything?"

"Some is in Cassidy's new room," Kate said. "The rest is in the attic or garage."

"That must have been a lot of work."

"I hired someone to unpack and move the boxes."

As she always did whenever something needed to be done. Kate ran an efficient household for someone who worked sixty plus hours a week.

Cassidy clicked her tongue. Her eyes widened and she made the same clicking sound again. And again. And again.

His gaze returned to the living room. Same couch and coffee table, but the walls... "You painted."

"Last month, I did some updating to the interior."

Tension from the past week crept into his shoulders. Update her life, update her house. Jared tried not to take the change personally. They were talking a new paint color, not a new man. "The blue is nice."

Kate raised her chin. "I thought so."

The challenge in her tone made Jared take a closer look at the living room. The paint wasn't the only difference. Their wedding portrait had been removed, and new pictures, framed and matted botanical prints in black frames, hung on the wall. The multicolored patterned rug they'd picked out one rainy afternoon at Pottery Barn had been replaced with a straw looking mat. And the bookshelves seemed less full. Were his books missing?

"What do you think?" she asked.

"A lot of changes." Jared felt strange as if she'd taken their home and made it all hers. He didn't like that. Or the differences. Yes, they had been planning to get divorced, but couldn't she have waited until the dissolution was final? Unless she'd already divorced him in her heart and the paperwork was just a formality. He shrugged off the idea. He couldn't believe that was true, not when he remembered what they'd had. He would woo Kate back. He would win her heart. "Where's our wedding picture?"

"I'm having the frame changed to match the blue better."

Okay, good. She was fitting the idea of their married life into her new room, not throwing the old away altogether.

The baby yawned.

He shifted her in his arms. "Are you tired, Cassidy?"

"Baaaah," she replied and stuck her fingers in her mouth.

"Don't be fooled," Kate said. "She's only lulling you into complacency."

"She's a baby."

"She's a smart baby who won't sleep.

Jared laughed. "Tonight will be the night."

He wished.

Kate rolled her eyes. "In your dreams."

His dreams revolved around his wife, not Cassidy. He'd missed making Kate smile. "Wait and see."

"I will."

The baby's eyelids fluttered shut then sprung open.

Kate crossed her arms. "Told you so."

"Patience." He rocked Cassidy and kissed her head above the bandage. "Isn't that right, sleepyhead?"

"You're not giving up?" Kate asked.

"Never. It's called perseverance."

"Or stubbornness."

"As long as I win—" he stared at the sleeping baby in his arms "—and I just did. It worked."

"No."

"See for yourself," he whispered.

"You've got the touch that's for sure," Kate said, and he hoped he'd get to use that touch on her. "Now can you make the transfer to her crib without waking her up?"

He wasn't at all sure he could. But with Kate smiling at him, teasing him, reminding him of what they'd once shared, he was willing to try.

Jared winked. "Watch the master."

"Where do I buy a ticket?"

The amused gleam in her eyes lit a spark in Jared. Maybe once he put Cassidy to bed, Kate would let him tuck her in, too.

Kate stood in the doorway of Cassidy's room and watched Jared in action. Wearing a navy suit, light blue dress shirt and blue striped tie, he looked more like a Hugo Boss model than a new father. Yet his daddy instincts were spot-on. She found that incredibly attractive as well as a tad bothersome. A tiny part—one Kate hated to admit—resented him for succeeding where she had failed.

As Jared gently placed Cassidy in the crib, Kate held her breath. This was where the baby always woke up with her. Yet Cassidy remained asleep. Again, Kate didn't get it. Sure, he'd baby-sat before, but he'd never had to do anything like this. Still Jared acted as if he'd done this a million times as if he'd been a dad for a really long time.

He quietly backed out of the room. "Mission accomplished."

The guy must have an angel on his shoulder or made a

pact with the devil. He never lost when he set his mind to something. Even, Kate realized, their divorce. He was getting his way. As usual.

Darn him.

For a second she felt like kicking the door or making some other loud noise, but common sense took over. Or maybe self-preservation. A block of uninterrupted sleep would make all the difference for her fatigued body and brain. With some rest, she could finally be the mother she wanted to be.

"If I didn't know better," Kate whispered, "I'd think the two of you were in cahoots."

"It's been that bad?" Jared asked.

She didn't want to admit the problems she'd had this week. "Bad might be a bit extreme."

"Let's go downstairs and talk so we don't wake Cassidy," he said. "It's been a while since I've been home."

Kate remembered the last time he'd returned from a business trip on a Friday night. She'd helped him undress, relishing in the scent of him and not caring whether the buttons on his shirt remained attached or not. They'd tumbled into the bed and knocked over the nightstand. And then they'd... She took a deep breath. Looking as handsome as Jared did tonight, she'd better put those memories behind her once and for all.

Pretending to be in love when they hardly saw each other had been easy. She didn't want to fall into the same trap again.

In the kitchen, Kate pulled a brown paper bag from the refrigerator. "If you're hungry, I bought you a sandwich from the deli."

He took the bag with a chuckle. "Thanks."

"What's so funny?" she asked.

"I didn't expect dinner tonight."

"What were you hoping for?"

"A cup of coffee and, maybe, a smile."

Thank goodness he hadn't wanted sex. Relieved, she grinned. "You hit the jackpot. You got the smile and I already brewed a pot of decaf. Though I have beer if you want one of those."

"After all that crying, a shot of whiskey might not be so bad." He took off his jacket, sat on one of the bar stools at the breakfast bar and unwrapped his turkey and provolone sandwich. "But a cup of decaf will be great. Thanks."

"You're welcome."

See. They could be pleasant and platonic. No problem. This might actual work. Of course once they started seeing other people... No, she didn't want to think about that.

He loosened his tie. "Would asking for dessert be pushing it?"

Kate removed two mugs from the cupboard. The cups, white with mini blue coffee mugs painted all over them, had been a wedding gift from one of his co-workers. She'd boxed them up, trying to put all reminders of their marriage away, but this week Kate decided to unpack them. Removing all the reminders of Jared from the house might upset him. "It depends on what you want and whether I have any to give you."

He rolled up his sleeves. "I want..."

Uh-oh. The desire in his eyes made her feel like she was the only dessert he wanted. He smiled, complete with dimples. Her heart hammered against her chest. Oh, boy. His smile was better than she remembered. Kate looked away, but she could still feel his gaze on her and see those dimples. She was in so much trouble.

"Cookies," he said finally.

"Cookies," she repeated, trying to regain control of her raging hormones. "I have a bag of Oreos in the pantry."

"Another one of my favorites."

She didn't want him to think she had gone to any special trouble. Sure, she'd purchased a few of his favorite foods, but that was common courtesy. Nothing more. She poured coffee into the two cups. "Well, I knew you were coming."

"You're the perfect hostess."

That was her intention.

"Here you go." As Kate handed him one of the steaming mugs, her arm brushed his hand. Accidental, but she felt a burst of heat at the spot of contact. Distance. She needed to get away from him. She went to the pantry and pulled out a bottle of vanilla flavored syrup and the bag of cookies.

"Thank you," he said.

She wouldn't meet his eyes.

"Something wrong, Kate?"

You. That wasn't correct. Her own feelings were the problem. "Nothing's wrong."

He took a sip. "Perfect."

He liked his coffee strong and black. He wasn't the type for sugar or cream or flavored syrups. She added a shot of vanilla into her cup. "Someday you'll join the rest of us and drink lattes and mochas."

"Never."

And he was probably right. Jared and his entire family stuck to traditions. Big ones, like naming children after older relatives, and small ones, like how they took their coffee. She, on the other hand, had zero family traditions unless you counted eating Thai food while watching the Academy Awards every year.

Kate wouldn't mind acting out a love scene with Jared. The thought melted her insides like butter. Not good. Shivering, she wrapped her hands around her mug.

"Are you cold?" he asked.

Actually she was quite warm. Okay, hot. "I'm fine."

"So have you talked to the pediatrician about this not-sleeping-hold-me-all-the-time problem?" he asked.

Good, maybe if they talked about the baby she could stop thinking of him as a, well, a man. One who she wanted to touch her again. "I'm not sure I'd call it a problem, but no, I haven't."

"What about my parents?" He picked up his sandwich. "Does she act the same way at their house?"

"Cassidy has no problem napping there during the day, but when she's here at night, sleep becomes a foreign word."

"Her internal clock might be screwed up."

"I don't think so. Susan would have mentioned something like that. I remember when she told me the baby had started sleeping at least four hours at a stretch during the night. She said she felt like a new woman."

"Maybe Cassidy's gotten spoiled," he suggested. "At the hospital she had round-the-clock care and attention."

"The books say you can't spoil a baby." Besides Kate couldn't spoil her if she wanted. Not working all day. "Why all the questions?"

His interest confused her. Jared, like all the male Reeds, might hold the babies during family get-togethers, but they never joined in the baby talk.

"I need to know what's going on," he said.

So he took the new responsibility seriously. Kate wondered whether his caring dad act was well, an act. She was surprised, but happy to discover he did care.

"I don't think that's the problem with Cassidy," Kate said. "She's lost her parents, spends her days at one house and her nights at another. That's a lot to take in for a baby."

Too much? Guilt slithered up her spine.

Jared wiped his mouth with a napkin. "Maybe she'll be better now that we're all here together."

Kate's muscles knotted. They were only together for a couple of days. And then the situation would change. Again. "One can hope."

"Yes, one can." Mischief glinted in his gaze. "So where am I sleeping tonight?"

His suggestive tone made her set her cup on the counter before her unsteady hand dropped it. "You're sleeping in the guest bedroom."

Jared didn't say anything, but his eyes darkened. He couldn't be surprised. Upset, maybe. But this was what they'd agreed upon. The rules they'd set.

And ones they would stick to. No matter what.

She expected him to say something. He didn't. And the silence magnified the stress between them. Kate could fix that.

"I had the room cleaned out, including the armoire." She refilled his mug, hoping her words didn't sound as lame as she thought they did. "I had pictures hung on the wall, too."

As if Jared would care.

He took another bite of his sandwich.

"All you're missing is a dresser." She wanted to keep the silence from returning. "We can buy one this weekend."

His gaze focused on her, and her pulse skittered. "You've thought of everything."

The tone of his voice told her he hadn't meant the words as a compliment. "I, um, tried."

Because that's what Kate did. Considered all the possibilities. Made plans for all the contingencies. Or at least she had until…tonight.

Jared had thrown her—not to mention her hormones—for a loop. And that left her worried about what the rest of the weekend would hold.

Maybe she was the one who needed that shot of whiskey.

Or better yet, an entire bottle.

So much for there being no place like home. Right now, being home pretty much sucked. His new room was small—eight by nine if he were being generous—without a closet. Without his wife.

Lying on a full-size mattress with his feet hanging over the edge, Jared glanced at the clock. Midnight. Sleeping wasn't easy when his wife, the woman he hadn't slept with in two months and twenty-three days, was sleeping down the hall. Alone. In a king-size bed. Probably wearing some short little nightshirt that had ridden up the curve of her hips. He missed touching her soft skin, feeling her warm body pressed against his in a perfect fit.

As he calculated ways to make Kate fall for him all over again, his eyelids grew heavy. He'd been on East Coast time all week, and the time difference was catching up to him. He rolled over. Sleep came fast and hard.

A cry shattered the silence of the house like a rooster's call at dawn. He looked at the clock. Two. Another cry.

Cassidy.

He scrambled out of bed, hit his calf on his luggage and hurried to her room. But Kate had beat him there.

A small lamp provided a dim light, enough for him to see her, wearing a nightshirt that showed off her long, slender legs, holding the baby.

"Let's get you a bottle, hungry girl," Kate said.

Hungry girl. If only Kate were saying she was hungry for him. He felt a twinge in his groin. The baby sobbed.

He concentrated on the task at hand. "Want some help?"

Kate sucked in a sharp breath. "I didn't hear you come in."

"Sorry." He yawned. "You want me to get the bottle?"

"I can do it." But instead of heading to the kitchen, she lowered the fussing baby to the changing table and pulled a diaper from the lower shelf.

"Let me change her," he offered, not wanting to replay the scene earlier tonight. "While you warm the bottle."

Kate unzipped Cassidy's pajamas.

"If we work together," he said. "We can get back to bed that much sooner."

Alone, together, he'd take what he could get at this hour.

"Cassidy needs to be changed." Kate strapped the baby to the table and handed him the diaper. For a moment they both held onto it, and then she looked away. "Everything is here, including a new sleeper if the one she's wearing is wet. I'll be back with the bottle."

Victory. She was actually letting him help.

He undid the diaper, and his satisfaction evaporated. Gross. He should have opted for the bottle.

After the diaper change, Jared rocked, swayed and walked Cassidy, but nothing made the baby happier or sleepy.

Kate returned with bottle in hand. "I can take her."

"You've been doing this all week." Jared reached for the bottle, purposely brushing his fingers against Kate's and watching her pull away her hand. So she felt the heat, the connection, too. Good. He placed the bottle in an eager Cassidy's mouth. "Go back to bed."

"Are you sure?" Kate said. "She doesn't go to sleep right away."

"All the more reason for you to grab some shuteye now."

She bit her lip. "Yell if you need me."

He needed her. Badly. But not in the way she was offering. But hey, at least she hadn't argued with him about this. A positive step. "I will."

With that, she left the room. He pictured her crawling into bed, sliding under the covers and her nightshirt riding up again. One peek was all he wanted.

Jared glanced at Cassidy, who sucked down her bottle as if it were a chocolate milkshake, not formula. "Let's see if you need to burp."

Once she'd burped, finished the bottle and burped again, Jared walked Cassidy to her crib. She fussed, tears falling from her eyes. "Do you want to rock?"

She answered him with a sigh.

Jared sat on the rocker he'd helped Brady refinish. Cassidy settled down for about five minutes until she cried again.

He walked around her room, and that seemed to do the trick. Until he stopped. The crying started again.

Now he understood what Kate had been talking about and why she looked exhausted. How had she done this every night without losing it? This was only his first night, and he was already tired of the routine and ready for sleep himself.

"It's late, baby." He walked more like a robot on automatic mode but the movement calmed Cassidy. "You had your bottle. Your diaper's clean. Time for nighty-night."

But Cassidy didn't seem to understand. Or maybe she didn't care. He respected Kate dealing with this and still managing to go to work each morning.

"I'll take over," a quiet voice said from behind him.

"Kate," he said surprised. "I thought you were asleep."

"I was, but woke up."

He wasn't about to accept defeat. And those rings under her eyes seemed darker. Jared wondered if she'd actually slept. And that upset him. She never wanted to give up control. "I can do this."

"I know, but tomorrow will be a long day if we're both tired." She reached for the baby, but he didn't let go. For a moment the three of them were locked together. Not quite a group hug, or passionate in any sense of the word, but he'd take it. "Really, Jared, get some sleep."

He heard the familiar determination in her voice. Stalemate. He couldn't count the number of times it had happened before. Arguing with her would only lead to a fight.

Jared let go. "I'm not going to be able to sleep knowing you're still awake."

"Then stay up," she said. "It's your choice."

As he walked to the opposite side of the room and leaned against the wall, Kate sang a quiet lullaby. Funny, but he'd never heard her sing except one time at karaoke. This was different. Love filled the sweet sound. Patience, too. Her song captivated him as did Kate herself.

She was a mom. Cassidy's mom.

They'd made the right choice for the baby. Jared knew

that without a doubt. He also knew something else. He needed Kate and Cassidy in his life, and they needed him, too. Kate just didn't realize it yet, but she would. He would show her just how much she needed him, stupid no sex rule or not.

CHAPTER SEVEN

CASSIDY usually woke up at six o'clock in the morning. This time, with Jared in the house, Kate wanted to be prepared.

At five-thirty, she showered and dressed, putting on gray pants, a pale pink blouse, pearl necklace and matching earrings. Perfect mom clothes, she thought. Kate brushed mineral powder foundation over her face, added a touch of blush and lip gloss. A bit early for a Saturday, but walking around in her nightshirt didn't seem like a smart idea. Especially after she'd noticed Jared checking out her legs last night. Thank goodness she'd shaved.

Not that she wanted him to find her attractive.

Kate didn't.

But she felt better knowing her legs looked good. At least, she hoped they had.

At precisely six o'clock, she sneaked a peek into Cassidy's room. The sight of an empty crib sent panic rolling through Kate. She struggled to breathe. "Cassidy."

"Downstairs," Jared called up.

Kate hurried down the stairs and into the kitchen. She skidded to a stop. Cassidy sat in her high chair, and Jared fed her from a bowl.

Kate's blood pressure spiraled. "What are you doing?"

"I'm feeding Cassidy her breakfast."

"She's not eating solids yet."

"There was a box of rice cereal in the pantry."

Kate placed her hands on her hips. "Your sister gave the box to your mother to give to me."

"I know," he said. "My mom told me."

"You called your mother?" Kate asked, though as soon as the question was out, she realized how stupid her words must sound. Jared talked to his family all the time. His parents, his sisters and brothers. Aunts, uncles and cousins, too.

"Yes, I called her. The bottle didn't seem to fill Cassidy up." Jared spooned more cereal into the baby's mouth. "Don't worry. After I talked with my mom, I double-checked the baby book on the counter. Solids are okay for four months olds."

"But they don't recommend starting solids until six months to alleviate allergies."

"Well, my mom fed us solids at four months and we turned out okay." Jared stuck another spoonful of rice cereal into the baby's open mouth. "Besides Cassidy likes it. Maybe she'll sleep longer with something more substantial in her stomach."

If they wanted to be perfect parents, they needed to stick to a plan. Not make changes as it suited them. "You should have asked me first. I was awake."

"You were in the shower," he said. "I could have come in, but I didn't think you'd appreciate that."

Okay, he was right about that. The thought of Jared walking into the steam-filled bathroom raised her temperature a few degrees. "You could have waited."

"Why?" he asked. "We are both her guardians, Kate.

Her parents, now. I realize you like things a certain way and you've spent more time with the baby than I have, but I need to be a part of this, too."

"You are a part of this."

"Am I?" he asked. "You could have slept last night and left Cassidy with me, but you didn't."

Okay, she'd give him that one. "You were tired, but stayed up, too."

"I'm only home a couple of nights a week." He wiped Cassidy's messy white face with her bib.

"A wet washcloth would work better," Kate offered.

He glared at her. "This is what I'm talking about."

"What?" Kate felt as if she had to defend herself. "I'm only trying to help. And I wanted to wait until Cassidy was six months to try solid foods because Susan had a peanut allergy. Cassidy could be more susceptible to food allergies."

"I didn't know," he said. Not much of an apology, but knowing Jared that's all she would get. "But if you're worried about allergies, we don't have to feed her anything else except rice cereal until she turns six months."

Kate didn't want to fight. They'd done too much arguing before they broke up. "I guess."

"If it's any consolation, Cassidy seems to like it. She's scarfing down the cereal like it's ice cream." He made a face. "Don't know why. The stuff tastes pretty bland."

"You tried it?"

Jared nodded. "Isn't that what you're supposed to do when you're a parent?"

"I have no idea, but I've never seen that in any of the baby books."

"Maybe you need to stop relying on the baby books."

His suggestion brought a flash of hurt. Jared could always call on his family for help, but with their strange marriage arrangement, she hadn't felt comfortable doing the same. His family did enough caring for Cassidy during the week. Besides, Kate didn't want to appear incompetent. "And do what instead?"

He raised a brow. "Try winging it."

The concept went against every one of Kate's instincts. "I'm not sure that's a good idea."

Cassidy knocked the spoon with her hand. Rice cereal flew through the air and landed on Jared's face.

The baby squealed.

"Very funny, sweet pea." Laughing, he wiped his eyes with a napkin. "At least Cassidy seems to understand the definition of winging it."

Kate wanted to remain indifferent to him, and not care what he did, said or looked like. But at this moment indifference was the last thing she felt for Jared. Especially when he looked so adorable with splotches of cereal and a dimpled smile on his face. "You look—"

"Like a clown?"

"No."

"A papier mâché model?"

"Close, but no, you look like a dad." She grabbed a paper towel, wet it and wiped his face clean. "The kind who all the kids in the neighborhood will want to play with."

"What about you?"

She swallowed. "Me?

"Would you want to play, too?" he asked.

Oh, yes. Kate met his warm, intent gaze, her heart thudding.

Oh, no.

* * *

Winging it worked great, Jared thought smugly a few hours later. As they walked around the neighborhood full of cozy bungalows and English-style cottages on the partially cloudy May morning, Cassidy fell asleep in her stroller without so much as a peep. Maybe they'd finally learned the secret to naptime—keep the baby away from the crib.

"So…Chinese takeout, barbecue or pizza for dinner?" Kate asked.

"Whatever would be easiest," he said.

Walking with Kate, talking with Kate reminded him of when they'd first got married and would stroll through the tree-lined sidewalks hand in hand and catch up on their week. Except this afternoon they pushed a stroller, kept their distance from each other and avoided any source of controversy with their conversation topic. No work talk, only food talk.

"Pizza would be the easiest," Kate said after they'd gone around and around, about various restaurants and the block. "Pepperoni and mushroom."

His favorite.

"Don't you like olives and sausage?" he asked. "On a thick crust?"

She nodded. "But you like thin."

They were trying so hard to get along. Maybe too hard.

But he understood the reasoning. If they were polite and nice, they could pretend no underlying passion and heat brewed between them. Of course maybe he should just admit he was too tired to do anything but be a good boy and follow the rules. "Let's order a regular crust."

"Sounds good," she said.

But good wasn't enough for him. He wanted things

back to the way they were. Even though they were
outside, the atmosphere, like the conversation, felt forced
and strained. He didn't like that. But focusing on the
negatives wouldn't help, Jared realized. Bottom line—
they were together. They were a family. Perhaps not a
totally functional one, but even this much had to be
enough for now.

He noticed an empty lot on the corner. "What happened
to the Pahls's house?"

"Someone bought the house and tore it down," Kate
said. "The land was worth way more than the structure."

On that one intersection alone, a house was for sale, one
had been demolished, another was being remodeled and a
fourth had been primed for a paint job. "Things are
changing," Jared said. "I've noticed more traffic from non-
locals."

"True, there are more cars on the streets, but our
property value has gone up." She sounded pleased. "It's
that old saying—location, location, location."

"I always thought the location was great."

"Now others agree with you." Kate's mood seemed to
improve. "It makes financial sense to do the remodel."

And give them more space, another bathroom and an
updated kitchen.

"I think we should still hold off." Jared didn't want
them to live in Portland, but he couldn't tell that to Kate.
"Too many changes at one time—"

"Would be too much for all of us," she finished for
him.

There it was again. That feeling of oneness. Strain,
stress, whatever else that kept them apart couldn't hide the
bond between them. She *had* to feel the connection, too,

and Jared suppressed his guilt over keeping quiet about his real reason for not wanting to pour money into the house.

Back home while Kate fixed lunch, Jared read board books to the baby. After lunch, they played with Cassidy under her floor gym. Sure, tension remained between him and Kate, but nothing had gone wrong as far as the baby was concerned. No need to refer to any baby books or Google information on the Internet. He and Kate were getting parenting down and that felt great.

"It's afternoon naptime," he said, holding Cassidy on his lap. "My mom says the baby takes two naps at her house."

"Why don't we take her on another walk?" Kate suggested. "She can fall asleep and we'll get some exercise."

"You said she was dealing with a bunch of changes. Maybe we should try to keep to her routine at my parents' house."

"You're right."

Her dubious tone made him smile. He rose, ready for the challenge. "Then let's do it."

"I can put her down."

"So can I."

Impasse. Again.

Only this time, Jared held the prize. That meant he won. "Since I've got her, I'll put her down."

"I've got your back covered."

He laughed. "You sound like we're going to war."

"Don't you remember last night?" she asked.

"It wasn't that bad." He carried Cassidy up the stairs. "It's time for your nap, baby. Show us how well you can go to sleep on your own."

The baby gooed.

"That's right," he said. "Show us how tired you are, sleepyhead."

Kate followed him up the stairs. "I wouldn't talk too much or get her excited in any way."

"So I shouldn't tickle her toesies?"

"I wouldn't recommend it."

"What about yours?" he asked.

"Well—" her mouth curved "—this probably isn't the best time."

But she hadn't said no. Progress.

"Right now we should just put the baby to bed," Kate said.

Jared changed Cassidy's diaper and carried her to the crib. He kissed the top of her head, just above the white bandage. "Sleep well, princess."

Mommy and Daddy need some more alone time.

He lay the baby in the crib. Wide-eyed and innocent, she gazed up at him with her big blue eyes, and she wailed. The blood-curling scream made every single one of his nerve endings stand at attention like Buckingham Palace guards.

"Pick her up," Kate said, rushing to the crib.

"No." He patted Cassidy's back. "We're here, baby, but you need to go to sleep."

The baby's face turned red, and tears shot from her eyes.

Clutching the crib rail, Kate's knuckles went white. "This isn't working for me."

Him, either. "Give it—"

"Shhh." She picked the baby up. "Don't cry, sweetie. We're here."

A minute.

Cassidy rested her head on Kate's shoulder, held onto Kate's hair with one hand and cried.

The minutes passed slower than the concession lines on opening day. With every tear the baby shed, Jared felt his composure unraveling. After thirty minutes of the baby's tantrum, he wanted to scream himself.

"I can't take this much longer," he said finally.

"I know, but I'm not sure what else to try."

Swaying hadn't worked. Rocking, either.

He had to give Kate credit. Her voice remained calm. She kept in constant motion even though she looked ready to fall asleep herself at any minute.

"We've got to figure this out and make her stop," he said. Before Cassidy's naptime behavior pushed he and Kate over the edge. They had enough problems on their own to work out. They didn't need this, too. "I'm going downstairs."

"For what?" she asked.

"To check the baby books."

Kate sat on the rocking chair for the third time. She arched her eyebrows, but her smile was sympathetic. "What happened to winging it?"

He shrugged. "So I'm an idiot."

"No, you're a new parent, that's all," she said with the understanding of a mom. "It's not as easy as you think it will be."

"You're right," he admitted. "I don't know how you managed on your own."

"You do what you have to do."

Exactly. And Jared wasn't going to let a tiny baby defeat them. A man on a mission, he stormed downstairs. Thumbing through the stack of baby books on the table, he ran through all the checklists with flowcharts and what-if scenarios. Nothing explained why Cassidy hated going to sleep so much. Nothing told him what to do.

So he did what any other man would do in this situation. He picked up the telephone and called his mother.

"I don't know what the problem is, dear," Margery, mother of five and grandmother of seven, said. "Cassidy has no problem going down for a nap in the morning and in the afternoon here. Have you checked her temperature?"

Jared hung up the phone, feeling worse than before, and returned to Cassidy's room. "Where's the thermometer?"

Kate walked the perimeter of the room with the baby in her arms. "She doesn't feel warm."

"Just tell me where it is?"

She patted a sobbing Cassidy. "In the hall bathroom. Second drawer."

A minute later, he ran the thermometer over the unbandaged portion of her forehead, but the reading was way too low. What little remained of his tired spirits disappeared completely.

"Hold the button down as you scan," Kate explained kindly. "You'll hear double-beeps when it's finished."

"Thank you." Jared hoped he sounded sincere, not irritated like he really felt. This wasn't Kate's fault. She was trying to help him. The way he wanted to help her.

He scanned the baby's forehead again, and this time the device worked. The action, however, aggravated Cassidy more, but he kept going. If she had a fever, they could fix that. At the double-beep, he checked the readout. His entire body seemed to sag. "No fever."

A good thing, really, but no temperature meant he had to keep looking for the reason she acted this way.

"What do you want to try next?" Kate asked.

"I'm out of ideas." Jared patted her shoulder. "I just can't believe you did this all yourself."

"I only had to deal with nighttime, not naptime."

That was enough. And earned his undying respect and admiration. "I'm still impressed."

"Thanks."

"So do you have any other ideas?" he asked.

She gave a half smile. "Are you up for another walk?"

As Kate hoped would happen, the afternoon stroll around the neighborhood worked. Cassidy fell asleep in her stroller as soon as they reached the end of the street, but by nine o'clock that night, she threw another tantrum. Cassidy did not want to go to bed. Again. It was too dark and late for another walk. Not that Kate had the inclination or the energy to take the baby out once more. Thank goodness Jared was here because she could not take any more. Physically exhausted and emotionally drained, she collapsed on her bed.

She had no idea how Susan had done this. Her friend may have spoken about being tired or wanting to lose weight, but she had never complained about the baby. And that was all Kate had wanted to do today.

"We should wave the white flag and surrender," she yelled to Jared, who walked Cassidy in the hallway. "Maybe then she'll stop crying."

Though Kate doubted it. She crawled under the covers as if the cotton blanket could shield her from the baby's latest fit. Anything for a reprieve.

Cassidy sobbed.

Jared walked into the room and sat on the bed. "I think we're reaching the saturation stage."

The baby hiccupped.

Kate felt light-headed from the fatigue of trying to get the baby to sleep. "I'll take over, but I'm going to need some help getting up."

"Mind if we join you instead?" Jared asked.

Anything to stay in bed. Staring at the ceiling, she patted the space next to her. "Please do."

He placed the baby in the center of the king-size bed so Cassidy lay between them. "Why don't we rest for a little bit?"

Rest. The word was ambrosia to Kate's ears. And then she realized she had invited Jared into her bed. Her body tensed. What had she been thinking? She hadn't. That was the problem. Biting her lip, she tried to control her erratic pulse.

"That means you, too, baby," he said.

Cassidy's tears stopped, as if she realized she'd won another round, and she cooed.

The baby. Kate's worry was premature. Cassidy would keep anything from happening between her and Jared. Of course, if Kate stuck to the rules, nothing would happen anyway.

"She likes this bed," Jared said. "Just not her own."

"I don't understand." Kate rolled on her side so she faced the now content baby and a relieved Jared. "How could this cute little girl also be the crying crib monster?"

Cassidy reached into the air with her arms and kicked her yellow footie clad feet.

He laughed. "I don't know, but she's happy."

"Yes," Kate said. She wished she felt happy, too, but she only felt…stressed. Especially the way Jared's shirt tightened across his chest and the muscles on his arms as he lay on his side. She swallowed.

Peals of laughter escaped from the baby's mouth.

"This sure beats tears," Kate said, trying to sound cheerful. And not stare at him.

"Too bad it's not always like this," Jared said.

He meant Cassidy. He had to mean Cassidy. Kate wet her lips. "Maybe we've reached a crossroad."

His gaze locked on hers. "I hope so."

Jared reached his hand across the pillows and touched her head. Kate stiffened, unsure what to say, but knowing she couldn't allow him to touch her. Not like this. In bed. Together.

He combed his fingers through her hair, and her body went limp. She couldn't help herself. Having him touch her felt so good and so right. And that was so wrong. But Kate didn't want to think about all the reasons she should stop him. She wanted to enjoy this a few minutes longer.

All these months sleeping alone, she'd forgotten how good having him in bed with her again felt. Kate almost sighed. "If you keep that up, I'm going to fall asleep."

"That will make two of you," he said softly.

The sight of Cassidy's closed eyes and curved lips brought relief. Finally. Quiet.

"What if she wakes up?" Kate whispered, watching the baby's steady breaths.

He placed one of the shams between their feet. "With you blocking that side and me on this side and the pillow down there, Cassidy isn't going anywhere."

That meant neither was Jared. So many buts and what-ifs ran through Kate's mind. She was too tired to deal with them. Maybe in the morning they'd have to set new rules to deal with situations like this, but for now she'd just go with it.

Leaning over, Jared brushed his lips across hers. "Sleep well."

The kiss had been platonic—a gesture out of camaraderie. Saying good-night, that's all he'd been doing. She shouldn't read anything into the action. Too bad her throbbing lips hadn't gotten that memo. She forced herself not to touch them.

"Close your eyes, Kate."

She did, but that didn't stop the thoughts running through her head.

"Night Katie."

Kate waited for him to take his hand away. He didn't. O-kay. She cleared her dry throat. "Good night, Jared."

Except for sleeping in his own bed last night—albeit with Cassidy between him and Kate—the rest of the weekend didn't improve. Cassidy, a teeny, tiny, helpless baby, turned into a raging, demanding demon any time the crib was involved. Naptime and bedtime became battles. And Cassidy, by sheer willpower alone, had been victorious.

Kate didn't want to get Cassidy in the habit of sleeping with her, and he was onboard with that. He wanted to be the only person in bed with Kate.

But there were only so many walks a person could take and by Sunday night, Jared felt like a war zone refugee—sleepless, homeless, shell-shocked. He couldn't wait to get back to Seattle though he would miss Kate. His job, even during the most critical of times, had never been as hard as taking care of a baby. And he was ready for some R & R.

The only good to come out of this was he and Kate had become a team trying to get the baby to go to sleep without a World War III reaction.

Jared hated leaving her to deal with Cassidy. Kate was exhausted when he arrived. His visit had barely given her a respite. How would she survive another week of the Crib Demon routine on her own?

"I'm sorry I have to go," he said, watching Cassidy play under her floor gym.

"You have your job," Kate said evenly. "I understand."

Her understanding increased his guilt. "But we have to do something about Cassidy."

"I know." Frustration clouded Kate's pretty face. "She never does this at your parents' house."

"That's what my mom told me."

"Maybe Cassidy needs more consistency."

"Consistency?" he repeated.

"If Cassidy spent more time here during the day so this isn't only the place she comes to for a bottle, bath and bedtime, she might not have such a terrible reaction."

"That sounds like a good theory," he said. "But I don't think my parents would want to spend their days here."

"No, you're probably right."

He hated to see her so discouraged. "You mentioned maternity leave or a leave of absence."

"Yes, but I can't do that. I'm still trying to catch up from the time I spent in Boise." She bit her lip. "Things would fall apart."

Things were already falling apart. If she didn't get some sleep, if Cassidy didn't settle into her new home, Kate was going to make herself sick. "At the office, you mean."

She stuck out her chin. "Yes."

He should have known. Her career and her firm came first. Before her health, before their marriage, before Cassidy.

But that was unfair, he realized. Lots of new moms worked by choice or necessity. Kate was doing her best to juggle a demanding job during the day with a demanding baby during the night. In fact, she was doing a lot more than he was.

Jared took a deep breath. "Kate, you can't go on like this."

A long silence ensued.

"I'll be fine," she said. "I just need to quit running every time Cassidy makes a sound."

Kate sounded confident, and her plan made sense. But he didn't believe her. Ordinarily Jared would take Kate at her word and take off, but this time…he didn't want to leave.

He stared at his two girls. Something had to change or the happy future, the perfect family, he was striving for was never going to happen. He needed to step up to the plate and hit the grand slam. "I'll take time off from work and stay home with Cassidy."

Kate's mouth gaped. "What?"

"I'll use some of my vacation time and stay here." Jared couldn't believe he had thought of the idea let alone suggested it, but what choice did have if he wanted to do what was best for his family? "That should help Cassidy adjust quicker."

Kate stuck her tongue between her teeth. "You'd do that for the baby?"

"Not just for the baby. For you, too. For me," he added hastily when her mouth tightened. Kate never could accept his help. "I'd worry about you here alone."

"That is so thoughtful of you, but I've managed so far."

"You've done great, but remember what I said. We're in this together. I mean that, Kate."

Gratitude filled her eyes. And he knew he was making the right decision.

"I have to talk to my boss, but they managed without me while I was in Boise. I'm sure they can survive another week or two," he said. "I've accrued so many weeks of vacation. I don't think I've used any since our honeymoon and last week."

Which, thinking about it, was a pretty sad statement about his life. And their marriage.

She looked wistful. "There wasn't enough—"

"Time," he finished for her. "Remember Maui?"

She nodded. "How could I forget? We were at the airport ready to go."

And as quickly as that, the tentative rapport between them faded as old hurts, old conflicts surfaced. "I told you to turn off your cell phone."

"How was I to know my biggest client had been slapped with a class action lawsuit?"

"You wouldn't have known if you'd listened to me."

"I would have had to fly back anyway."

"You could have had someone else handle the situation."

"Situation? It was a crisis. My firm's reputation was on the line. I couldn't hand the client off to someone else and go on vacation." She brushed her hair behind her shoulder. "At least I got our money back unlike the trip to Cancún."

"Hey, I had no choice but to fly to New York. Boss's orders," he explained. "We were supposed to reschedule the trip, but then…"

"We never did."

And probably never would. Jared swallowed.

"There's not going to be a lot of time in the future for

big vacations so I might as well use the time now," he said. "As long as you don't mind me being here during the week, too."

"I won't mind you here," she said softly, making him wonder if she was having a change of heart about the two of them.

He hoped so. "I'll try not to get in your way."

They used to joke about being two planes passing in the night. Except for the week of Thanksgiving and the time between Christmas and New Year's, they rarely spent weeknights together due to travel schedules. At least they would only be working around one of their work schedules now.

A stay-at-home dad.

Temporarily, he assured himself. Just until they tamed the Crib Demon and he made sure Kate ate and slept. He could relieve her of the bedtime battles and make the next move in his game plan to win her back. He would quadruple the progress he'd made this morning. No doubt.

"I'll talk to my boss in the morning," Jared said.

"Having you here will be good for Cassidy."

His being here would be great for all three of them. Kate would realize that soon enough. Putting on his game face, he clapped his hands together. "Just call me Mr. Mom."

She smiled. "Somehow I never pictured us as Mr. Mom and Mrs. Dad."

"What about Mr. and Mrs. Jared Reed?" he challenged.

Her smile faded. "I don't think so."

"So what do you suggest?"

"Hmmm." She pressed her lips together and winked. "What about Mr. and Mrs. Kate Malone?"

CHAPTER EIGHT

WEDNESDAY evening, Kate turned the car from the alley onto her driveway in the back and noticed the lights on in the house.

Jared was here.

A strange mix of apprehension and relief flowed through her. Kate parked the new four-door Ford Freestyle in front of the garage housing her beloved silvery blue BMW Boxster. She turned off the engine, but remained in the car.

She was relieved to have Jared back. Bedtime with Cassidy had only gotten worse since he'd left on Sunday. But knowing he would be here day and night, for at least a week, maybe more, made Kate nervous and uncertain. Jared had been nothing but cooperative, trying to make this arrangement work, but she hated unpredictability. She hated not having control. And that's what she feared would happen with him here.

Cassidy squealed.

Kate glanced in the mirror and saw the baby's smiling face through another mirror attached to the back seat. Affection for the little one overflowed in her heart. Surely Cassidy and doing what Susan desired for her daughter would make Kate's struggles worthwhile. "Give me a minute, okay?"

The baby cooed.

She'd take that as a yes.

Staring across the backyard, she saw Jared in the kitchen. Fluttery sensations overtook her stomach. She clutched the steering wheel. The butterfly aviary fluttering in her tummy had nothing to do with apprehension, and everything to do with attraction.

Uh-oh. Maybe that was the real problem. The temptation having Jared around 24/7 would bring.

A bed-size lump of worry lodged in her throat.

She couldn't afford to be tempted. She couldn't do anything to upset the precarious relationship—make that situation—between them. Too much was at stake. She glanced in the mirror at Cassidy.

And Kate knew what she had to do.

She needed to encase her heart in armor to immune itself from him. From his good looks and witty charm, from his willingness to use his vacation time to care for a baby he hardly knew and to help his almost-but-not-quite-ex-wife make the transition from working woman to working mother.

She exhaled slowly.

Cassidy giggled, another happy sound, but Kate wasn't about to push the baby's good mood. She didn't want Jared's second homecoming to be filled with tears. That would happen soon enough when bedtime rolled around.

She exited the car, swung her laptop case strap over her shoulder and opened the baby's door. "Are you ready to get out?"

"Ah-goo," Cassidy said.

Kate repeated the sound. "That's your favorite word, isn't it?"

"Ah-goo."

She reached into the center of the back seat, removed Cassidy from the car seat and carried her to the back door that opened as if on cue.

The scents of basil and garlic drifted out. Her stomach growled. She hadn't eaten a real meal with all the food groups or drank a liquid without a heavy dose of caffeine since…Sunday. When Jared had been here last.

"Perfect timing," he announced as she stepped inside. "Dinner's almost ready."

"You cooked?" Silly question once she got a glimpse of the kitchen. Something red simmered on the stove. An empty pasta sauce jar, a bag of spaghetti noodles and a bottle of Chianti sat on the tile counter. Water boiled in a huge pot. Something—garlic bread, she hoped—baked in the oven.

Kate recalled the dinner she'd given him when he'd arrived last Friday evening—a cold sandwich—and felt bad she hadn't cooked a meal for him. Of course Jared hadn't been taking care of a baby while trying to fix dinner tonight, and she had done the best she could at the time. But Kate realized she should have had a meal prepared for him by a professional chef. That was what a perfect wife would have done. Next time…

"It smells delicious." Her nervousness in the car seemed silly. He'd cooked her dinner, not tried to seduce her. She glanced at the bottle of wine. No, she had nothing to worry about as long as he didn't offer to rub her back. Kate cleared her throat. "When did you get here?"

"Around three." He dumped the bag of pasta into the

boiling water and set the timer on the stove. "My boss wanted me in on a conference call this morning."

"Is he okay with you taking vacation time?"

Jared nodded. "He asked me to check in with him at the end of the week. I told him I'd probably be gone two weeks."

Two weeks. She could handle that if Jared could.

She noticed a bottle in the warmer. "For Cassidy?"

"It should be ready."

Kate set her briefcase on the floor and tested the temperature of the formula in the bottle. Perfect. She shouldn't be surprised. Not with the competence he'd already demonstrated tonight. "Thanks. You've thought of everything."

He smiled. "I gave it my best shot."

She sat at the kitchen table—set with plates, silverware, napkins and wineglasses—and fed the bottle to a hungry Cassidy. Kate had no idea what she'd expected when she walked in the door, but this—a scene out of an alternate reality 1950's television show—wasn't it.

Jared stirred the sauce with a wooden spoon. Amazing. She didn't know they had a wooden one. A satisfied grin formed on her lips. Sure he'd only cooked a dinner, but the care he'd gone to make her feel special. Cherished. A way she hadn't felt in a long time. And she liked it.

"Do you need any help?" she asked.

"Thanks, but I'm almost done."

As the baby slurped down her formula, Kate watched Jared. He checked the boiling noodles, lowered the heat on the bubbling sauce and removed the bread baking from the oven. He'd always been comfortable cooking, more so than her, but she'd never seen him look so...domestic. He seemed perfectly at home in the kitchen. Her kitchen. Their kitchen, now.

Unfamiliar heat burned deep within Kate. She pressed her toes against the hardwood floor. "I could get used to this."

He glanced her way. "You think?"

Uh-oh. She hadn't meant to say the words out loud. She nodded, when her answer was really "most definitely."

And that, Kate acknowledged, was a problem. She wanted to establish a stable home and a routine for Cassidy, but Kate knew better than to depend on the same for herself. She would only end up disappointed and heartbroken again. They'd agreed on a marriage of convenience, not a happily-ever-after.

She patted Cassidy on her back and a loud burp exploded from the baby.

"That's my girl." Jared stirred the sauce again. "You'll show up all the boys when you are older."

His words sounded like something a dad would say, especially his dad. Kate fed the rest of the bottle to the baby. "Your parents didn't mention you were back when I picked up Cassidy."

He sliced the garlic bread. "My parents don't know."

Kate fumbled with the baby's bottle. Jared told his family everything. Good news, bad news, silly news. Nothing was off-limits with the Reeds. "You haven't talked to them about this?"

"I wanted to speak to them in person," he said. "I'm telling them over breakfast tomorrow while you're at work."

Sparing her the inevitable recriminations. Kate appreciated that. Dropping the baby off in the morning and picking her up in the evening had gotten easier. Her discussions with his parents and siblings revolved around

Cassidy, but Kate still wasn't sure how to act around them. She burped Cassidy again. "Are you concerned about their reactions?"

"My mom won't have a problem with my being here, but my dad…" Jared placed the bread on a plate and covered it with foil. "He may have some issues."

In other words, Vesuvius—the family nickname for his father's temper—was going to blow.

Frank Reed was a throwback to the days of a man who expected a cocktail in his hand when he walked in the door and dinner at six o'clock on the dot no matter whether his wife, Margery, was nine months pregnant, fighting the flu or chasing after her brood of five children. Frank still couldn't understand why Kate hadn't moved to Seattle and had filed for divorce instead, so Jared taking over primary child care duties might not go over so well.

"What time are they expecting you?" Kate asked.

"Oh, I'm not going there." He dumped the pasta in a large bowl, poured the sauce on top and stirred the mixture with the spoon. "I invited them to come here."

Here. Tomorrow. Kate gulped, making a mental note to clean the house later. His parents hadn't been here in months, and she wanted everything perfect for them. "Why here?"

"Home field advantage."

Forget home being any advantage. His father wasn't swayed in the slightest.

Flipping pancakes on the stove, Jared realized cooking a meal for his father while telling him he was staying home with the baby hadn't been one of his smartest moves.

"People are going to call you Mr. Malone," Frank Reed said. "I can't believe you, with an MBA from Stanford, are going to spend your day changing dirty diapers, doing housework and cooking."

"That's what I did, Frank," Margery said before Jared could speak up. She fed Cassidy another spoonful of rice cereal. "You didn't have any complaints about me doing the same thing for the last forty-five years."

"You're a woman." Frank's nostrils flared. "That's your responsibility."

She shook her head. "Times have changed, Frank."

"Gah," Cassidy said.

"See." Margery smiled. "Cassidy agrees with me."

Frank harrumphed.

At least his mom was on his side. Jared knew she would talk some sense into his father, but he wasn't ready to give up himself. He transferred the pancakes to a plate. "Besides, Dad, we have a housecleaner. There's no need for me to scrub toilets or the floor. And I won't be cooking every night."

Frank grumbled under his breath. "It's abnormal for a man to stay home while his wife goes to work."

Jared carried the plate to the table.

His father frowned. "The next thing you know, he'll be wearing an apron."

"*He* is standing right here," Jared said. "Pancakes anyone?"

"I'll take a couple more," Frank said.

As he dished up two pancakes, Jared grimaced. His father might complain, but he wasn't above eating the food he'd cooked. Seconds, even.

"Don't forget, Dad." Jared sat at the table. "I didn't quit my job."

Though he'd lost a big opportunity with a longtime

client by taking time off, but he wasn't about to tell his parents or Kate about that. Whatever sacrifices he made would be worth it when he and Kate were together, living as husband and wife.

Frank added a pat of butter and poured maple syrup over his pancakes. "Are you being paid?"

"Full salary and benefits." The only thing missing were marital benefits, but he was going to work on those. Starting tonight if he got the chance.

"And when will you return to your job?" Frank asked.

"I don't know yet." Jared cut into his pancakes. "Probably two weeks."

The lines on his father's face deepened.

"Frank, this is a good thing," Margery said. "We'll not only get to see Cassidy, we'll get to see Jared, too."

"Does that mean you'll still bring her over?" Frank asked.

Jared nodded. "We want Cassidy to be comfortable at both places, but we need to establish a routine and get her used to sleeping in her own crib first."

His dad leaned back in his chair. "Why don't you let the baby stay with us all the time?"

Margery laughed. "So you can stay home all day with Cassidy, but not Jared?"

Frank puffed out his chest. "I'm retired. I've earned my keep."

"Your father has fallen in love with this little girl." His mother's tender gaze focused on Cassidy. "And so have I."

Jared could tell with the attention his parents paid to Cassidy while she ate. He wondered if they ever left her alone for a minute. They hadn't since they had arrived this morning. "We appreciate all you've done so far and will be doing for us after I go back to Seattle."

"You could always do this full-time," Margery suggested.

"Yeah, right," Jared and Frank said at the same time.

Margery shook her head. "What does Kate think about all this?"

"I've only been here a day." Jared thought about Kate's reaction to his offer, to her pleasure over the dinner last night and her concerns about his father's reaction. Forward steps, definitely. "But the weekend was…encouraging."

And if she allowed him back in the master bedroom again, things would be even better.

Margery leaned forward visibly curious about her children's lives, as usual. "So the weekend went well?"

"'Well' might be a tad optimistic." He picked up his coffee cup. "It's hard to work on being a couple when all our energy is spent on a baby who won't sleep and fusses and cries all the time."

His parents laughed.

"What?" Jared asked.

"Welcome to our world, dear." His mother's eyes twinkled. "Just multiply what you're going through by five."

"So is this what parenting is always going to be like?" Jared asked, unsure he wanted to hear the answer.

"They sleep eventually," Frank said.

"And cry less." Margery wiped a speck of cereal from Cassidy's chin. "But once you have kids, your world does tend to revolve around them. Finding time for romance, and each other, gets more difficult."

They'd had enough trouble with romance before Cassidy arrived. Jared ate his pancake. Somehow he and Kate needed to find time for each other.

"It helps maintain your perspective, not to mention your sanity, when you have a spouse who's there to share in all the ups and downs," Margery added.

He set his fork down. "I have Kate."

His parents both sipped from their coffee cups.

Their action put him on the defensive. Jared understood why they might feel like that—Kate had decided not to move to Seattle and she had been the one to file for divorce. But those things had to be forgotten. The sooner his family realized that, the better. "Kate and I are committed to raising Cassidy together."

"That's what you've said."

"We're going to make our marriage work," he added.

"We only want you to be happy." Margery placed her cup on the table. "And we'll do whatever we can to help you."

But they didn't believe the marriage would work. He could see the truth in their eyes and feel their skepticism in his heart. And that hurt. More than he wanted to admit.

He was not going to fail.

Jared set his chin. "You'll see."

And they would. Once Cassidy settled into a routine, once Kate came to accept his ongoing presence in their house, her bed and life, they would have the kind of partnership, the kind of marriage his parents were talking about.

He just hoped it happened soon.

Kate walked into the living room. Jared sat on the couch with the laundry basket at his feet and Cassidy in the bouncer on the floor. On the bottom of the television screen, stock symbols rolled by on the electronic ticker tape. If only Kate found the stock market more interesting, she could concentrate on something other than how relaxed and handsome Jared looked in his green polo shirt, khaki shorts and bare feet.

Forget her knees being like wet noodles. They were already at the Jell-O stage.

Oh, boy. She sucked in a breath. Not the reaction she'd hoped to have when she saw him next. Kate steadied herself by kicking off her sling backs and holding onto a nearby chair. "Hi there."

Jared looked up from the pink gingham crib sheet he was folding. Concern filled his eyes. "What are you doing home so early?"

Good question. She wished she had an equally good answer. "I, um, let everyone have the afternoon off."

He tossed the sheet into the basket. "Are you feeling okay?"

Funny, but a number of her employees had asked her the same question. "I'm feeling fine, a bit rested, too, since you took the middle of the night shift for me."

She'd wondered whether his plan to stay home with Cassidy would work, but today had been a near normal day for Kate. The familiarity reassured her after the panic and disarray of the last week and a half. She felt more like her old self and Sean Owens, her dedicated assistant, had commented on her "return." And Kate couldn't deny the results—a wonderful and productive day, make that two-third's day, at the office.

"So why did you let everyone go home early?" Jared asked.

"Because I wanted to go home." And see him and Cassidy. Kate couldn't remember the last time she'd left work early unless she was catching a flight for a business trip. "I didn't feel right leaving unless everyone could go home, too."

"You're one helluva boss, Kate."

She wasn't sure if that was a compliment or not. She walked over to Cassidy and sat on the floor next to her. "Hello, baby, did you have a good day?"

As drool rolled from Cassidy's mouth, the baby smiled. Kate knew she'd made the right decision to come home early.

"Tell us about your day," Jared said. "I need adult conversation desperately."

She looked at Jared and felt her heart go bumpity-bump.

"Kate?" he asked.

She checked out the toy bar hooked to the baby's bouncer. She spun the mirror around much to Cassidy's delight. "We signed a new client, beBuzz Sportswear."

"Congrats."

"Thanks." A feeling of exhilaration washed over Kate. She'd forgotten how nice sharing her accomplishment with someone other than her staff could be. Kate didn't have that many friends. Susan. A couple of girlfriends from college. The rest she'd met through Jared who had all taken his side when they broke up. "Today capped off a long and unsteady courtship."

"Sometimes those are the most fruitful."

"I hope you're right."

"Me, too," he said, his intense gaze on her.

She wondered if he was talking about her new client or the two of them.

"We should open a bottle of champagne and celebrate."

Sharing a bottle of bubbly might not be the smartest move when she couldn't keep her eyes off of him. She remembered the last time they'd shared a bottle of champagne. Strawberries and whipped cream had been involved. They'd had to buy new sheets. "I was thinking I could take you and Cassidy out to dinner instead."

Jared's surprised look brought a rush of uncertainty. His lack of response only intensified those feelings.

"Would you like to eat out tonight?" She kept her voice steady when her insides shook worse than those of a nervous schoolgirl asking a boy to a Sadie Hawkins dance. "Your choice of restaurant, but it's not like a date."

"A date would be against the rules."

He still hadn't answered her question. She tilted her chin. "Yes, but we could, um, consider it practice. For, um, later, if we…when we see other—"

"I'd like to go out to eat," he interrupted to her relief. "But I'm not sure Cassidy would want to go. Why don't we have my parents watch her? We'd probably enjoy ourselves more."

"True. But aren't we supposed to be establishing a routine for the baby?"

"You're right," he said, sounding disappointed.

"We could go out after she went to sleep," Kate suggested.

"I'll give them a call." He picked up the phone before she could say wait or better yet no. A minute later he hung up. "They'll be here at seven."

"I just hope we don't have to spend hours getting her to fall asleep."

"Cassidy took two naps in her crib today." Pride filled his voice.

"How did that happen?" Kate asked.

"My mom taught me the importance of a bedtime routine, not just a schedule, and something called a binky."

"A what?

"A pacifier." Jared smiled. "She figured we were using one since Cassidy took one so easily at her house."

Kate racked her brain. "I don't remember Susan using one."

"Would you have paid that close attention?"

"No, but I can't believe a pacifier made the difference."

"Not just the pacifier," he explained, refolding the crib sheet. "But having a set routine we follow every time we put her down. I was skeptical myself and she cried a little, but nothing like her never ending crib demon crying fits."

"Good job."

A shy smile curved his lips. "My mom gets the credit. I only offered an assist."

"I'll thank her when she gets here," Kate said. "Speaking of your mom, how did this morning go with your parents?"

"They enjoyed the pancakes."

"What did they think about you taking time off to be with Cassidy?" And me, a little voice in Kate's head whispered.

"My mother supports my decision." He folded a pink, trimmed dress. "She said I had evolved and become a man for the twenty-first century by putting the needs of my family ahead of my career goals."

"That's great."

Jared shrugged. "My father wasn't as pleased."

He tried to sound lighthearted, but Kate knew how much his father's opinion meant to Jared. "I'm sorry."

"He'll get over it."

Of course, his father would. Jared was the golden child, the son who never did wrong, never disappointed. Frank would never stay mad at him for long.

"If it's any consolation," Kate offered. "I agree with your mom. What you're doing for Cassidy is pretty incredible."

Jared's gaze held hers, and she had to force herself to breathe. "Thanks."

Kate hadn't done anything to deserve his thankfulness. Not really. And that made her feel bad. Useless.

Cassidy reached up. "Gah."

"Are you ready to get out?" Kate looked at the baby dressed in a pink and yellow jumper and did a double-take. "Oh, no."

She unhooked the strap holding the baby in the bouncer and lifted her out. "Did you and Cassidy go out today?"

"We walked to the store."

"Was she wearing this?" Kate asked, her frustration rising.

Jared studied the baby. "Is something wrong with what she's wearing?"

Kate stifled a groan. "Her outfit is on backward."

"The snaps go in the front," he said.

"In the back," she said.

"No, they don't."

"Yes, they do." She unsnapped the jumpsuit and showed him the tag. "They go in the back where this belongs, too."

Kate took off the baby's outfit and put in on the right way. "See."

A beat passed.

"No wonder all those women kept staring at us in the produce department. And I thought they were looking at me. Not Cassidy's clothes." Jared released a heavy sigh. "No doubt they were whispering about my inability to dress my baby, not my remarkable pecs."

The humor in his voice evaporated her frustration. She laughed. "Okay, so maybe Cassidy wearing her clothes backward isn't such a big deal."

"You think?" he asked.

Kate nodded, feeling stupid for almost ruining a pleasant afternoon. "Overreacting is probably my way of compensating for my lack of parenting skills and knowledge."

He feigned disbelief. "No."

"Yes." Kate stared at Cassidy's orange and blue socks. Not the ones she would have chosen to go with the baby's pink shoes and clothing, but the baby didn't have to coordinate from head to toe. At least not under Jared's watch. "I'll try harder."

"You already have." He stared at her. "You're doing a fantastic job, Kate."

"Thanks." His compliment meant the world to her. She needed to hear she was doing well, even if it wasn't a hundred percent true. "I've been feeling a bit like a lone wolf mom."

"You don't have to feel that way anymore, Katie," Jared said with a smile. "Daddy wolf is here to help."

"You taking the 2:00 a.m. wake-up last night was huge."

"Those are a daddy wolf's specialty. I just have to keep my howling at the moon to a minimum."

She laughed. Cassidy did the same.

"I doubt the baby would mind the howling," Kate said. "She loves mimicking sounds and would howl alongside you."

"You're probably right."

He howled.

Cassidy released a high pitch squeal.

"You don't have to worry about the baby when she's with me," Jared said seriously.

"I know." No matter how much Kate might want to run everything, doing so wouldn't be fair to Jared or good for their arrangement. They would both have to compromise to make the marriage work. "I will make a point not to interfere with what you do with Cassidy."

"And I'll do my best to dress her properly with the tag in the back." With a hopeful smile, he extended his arm. "Deal?"

Kate shook his hand. "Deal."

CHAPTER NINE

Deal?

The only deal Jared wanted to make with Kate was about her being his wife…for real. Sure, he was supposed to be patient. He'd only been in town one day. But each time he saw her, the pull grew stronger, as did the ache inside.

Now that she was sitting across from him with the candlelight flickering, he couldn't deny his need any longer.

He wanted her. Bad.

A waiter removed the plates from the linen covered table.

"I'm glad we went out tonight," Kate said, looking more beautiful than ever. Her shimmery blue dress matched the color of her eyes.

Good thing they were in a public place or Jared might be in trouble. Who was he kidding? He was already in trouble.

She looked at him expectantly, waiting for his response.

"Me, too," he said.

The way she casually tucked her hair behind her ears made her look younger, almost innocent. But the smoldering heat in her eyes was like a kick in the groin.

Couldn't she see sex wasn't the problem? Sex was the solution to their problems.

The air around them seemed electrified. He reached for his water glass. "We'll have to do this again."

Anything to bring that warmth to her smile and the radiant glow to her face.

Unless he found other ways of doing that. He grinned.

A spark of laughter danced in her eyes. "Especially if we can find another place as quiet as this one."

It wasn't quiet like a church, but the soft conversation from the other diners seemed like whispers compared to Cassidy's chattering and crying. "You noticed that, too?"

She nodded.

"It's amazing how much noise one baby can make."

"Cassidy talks back to her bottle when she's drinking her formula," Kate said. "But I'm getting used to the racket."

"I'm going to need a few more days before I can say the same."

"It won't be easy, and there will be a transition period, but give it time. You'll get there and things will be fine."

Interesting. That sounded like his game plan for winning Kate back.

"I hope you know how much I appreciate you taking time off from work." She smiled shyly. "It's pretty incredible what you're doing."

Her words made him feel ten feet tall, but he wanted to give credit to her, too. "You're the one who's incredible, Kate. I'm amazed at how much you've done with Cassidy. You can handle anything."

"I still have a lot to learn, but thanks." Kate's eyes softened. "It's kind of strange, but sometimes I think I hear Cassidy crying when I'm at work."

"That's not strange, you've changed."

"Changed how?"

"Look at what you did today. You gave your employees the afternoon off, and you came home early yourself. When was the last time that happened?"

"Never."

"I bet it won't be the last time." He saw his future. Kate, Cassidy, more babies. "You're a mom, now. You've learned to be more flexible, not so set in your ways."

"Everything just feels so different."

The anxiety in her voice coupled with her sudden interest in the salt and pepper shakers suggested she wasn't only talking about the baby. "What do you mean?"

"Tonight. Being here with you." She toyed with her napkin. "I can't remember the last time you and I had a meal together in the middle of the week."

"Burgers in Boise."

"I meant here at home. Before."

Before the separation. Jared thought back and came up blank. But that wasn't surprising given their work schedules. "Dinner out on a Wednesday night is a lot more satisfying than a call from a hotel room."

"I agree," she said. "We'll have to make the most of the time while we can. Once you go back to work…"

It would be back to phone calls. He tried to reassure her. And himself. "We'll figure something out. Video calling. You'll think I'm right here with you."

"Except I'll be the one taking out the garbage."

"Builds muscles," Jared teased. "But I just got here yesterday. Let's not think about me going away already."

The sommelier approached with two flutes containing champagne. "I hear you are celebrating a special occasion."

Jared nodded. "My wife is."

Kate gave him the arched eyebrow what-are-you-doing look.

He leaned forward. "You never said no to champagne."

"But the baby—"

"Is asleep," he said. "My parents would have called if something was wrong. I only ordered us each a glass, not an entire bottle."

The sommelier waited patiently.

Kate smiled at the wine steward. "Thank you so much. I do enjoy a glass of celebratory bubbly."

"My pleasure." The sommelier placed the glasses on the table and bowed. "Enjoy."

Once the man walked away, Jared raised his champagne. "To a successful partnership."

"And a lasting one."

He hoped she wasn't only talking about her new client.

She tapped her flute against his. The chime of the crystal hung in the air like the song of a bird on a sunny day.

As she sipped her champagne, she seemed uncertain, a little nervous.

"Is something wrong?" he asked.

Her cheeks flushed. She set her glass down. "No."

He didn't believe her. Definitely a new Kate, and one he liked.

The waiter arrived with an order of profiteroles with two forks, a cappuccino for Kate and a cup of decaf for him.

"Profiteroles are my absolute favorite." She stared at the ice-cream filled pastry puffs sprinkled with powder sugar and drizzled with chocolate syrup. Jared wished she'd look at him with the same desire. "You're spoiling me."

That was the point. "I'm only getting started."

"Promises. Promises."

She would see soon enough.

He scooped a bite onto his fork and brought the taste toward her mouth. "For you."

Temptation flashed across her face, but caution tempered it. "I don't think this is such a good idea."

"The rules."

She nodded.

Screw the rules. He wanted to feed his wife.

"Come on, baby." He brought the fork closer. "Show me the tunnel so the choo-choo can come inside."

A relaxed smile formed. "It's a hangar and the plane needs to go inside."

"Open up."

She did. He placed his fork inside her mouth and her lips closed around it. "Mmm."

Talk about sexy.

Slowly he pulled the fork from her mouth. "Was it good for you?"

She laughed, the melodic sound wrapping around his heart. "Delicious."

He agreed.

A drop of chocolate sauce hung on her lower lip. As the pink tip of her tongue darted out to wipe it away, Jared's temperature skyrocketed. Sweet torture. He wanted a taste himself.

As Kate ate more of the dessert, the waiter brought the check. Jared reached for the bill, but Kate was faster.

"It's my turn," he said.

When they used to go out, each would take turns paying.

"You can pay for the champagne and dessert," she said. "But I invited you. I want dinner to be my treat."

He didn't want to spoil the night by insisting on picking up the tab. With a shrug, he handed her cash to cover his portion. "Thank you for dinner, but I hope you know I'm not an easy date."

The corners of her eyes crinkled. "I'll try not to be too disappointed."

He cocked a brow and did his best Latin lover impersonation. "But for you, baby, I could make an exception."

Laughing, she placed her credit card inside the leather-covered folder. The waiter promptly took the bill away.

Kate ate another bite of the dessert and wiped her mouth. "Thank you for the dessert, Jared. And the champagne. I really appreciate your support."

"You deserve it."

"Lots of people worked on winning the beBuzz account."

"I'm not just talking about your firm signing a new client, Katie."

She glanced up. "What then?"

"Cassidy."

"I'm only doing what anyone else would do if their best friend died." Eyes glistening, she looked up and blinked. "Besides, Cassidy is so easy to love. Even if she won't sleep at night."

Her humility touched him. He reached across the table and took hold of her hand, thin yet strong like the woman herself. "You've opened your heart and your life to the baby. You've become a mom. You've surprised me, my family, no doubt everyone else you know."

She bit her lip. "I never said I didn't want children."

"No, you didn't," Jared admitted. "But saying you wanted a family and then putting off getting pregnant made me wonder."

"I'm sorry. I didn't mean to send mixed signals."

"Me, either." He squeezed her hand. "You're a wonderful mother and a beautiful woman. I'm so proud you are my wife."

The gratitude shining in her eyes took his breath away.

The waiter returned with the bill. Kate pulled her hand from Jared's so she could fill out the charge slip. She placed the pen inside the folder and her napkin on the table.

"Finished?" he asked.

Kate nodded. "I'm ready to go home."

Home. Their home.

Maybe tonight would be the turning point. The start of their having a real marriage…

Anticipation rippled through him. If she desired him that meant she still loved him.

He stood and pulled her chair out. As they walked out of the restaurant, he placed his hand on the small of her back. She didn't stiffen; her muscles didn't tense. A good sign.

"Thank you, Jared. Tonight was really…special. I wish I could do something in return."

"You can," he said.

"What?"

Jared unlocked the car, opened her door and helped her into the seat. "You were never an easy date, either, but…"

Her eyes narrowed. "But what?"

Grinning, he walked to his side and slid into the seat beside her. "I wouldn't turn down a good-night kiss."

"A kiss?" She didn't sound horrified. More…intrigued. "This isn't a real date."

Could've fooled him. He locked his seat belt into place. "Not a date kiss. A slow, hot, take your breath away date kiss wouldn't be appropriate."

"Not appropriate at all." Kate shifted in her seat. "What kind of kiss are you talking about then?"

"A kiss between friends," he said. "That's all."

"To get us back in the game so to speak."

"Exactly."

"O-kay." She leaned over and kissed him lightly on the lips. The fresh scent of her surrounded him, making him heady. Her mouth lingering an instant longer than any other kiss from a friend he'd experienced ignited a fire inside him. His boiling blood pushed him toward the edge.

He was ready to jump. She only had to say the word.

"Friendly enough for you?" she asked with a slow, seductive smile. The woman didn't have an innocent bone in her body. Kate knew exactly where she wanted him. And had him.

Jared cleared his throat. "Yes. Very friendly."

He was definitely back in the game and so was she. Now all he had to do was to convince Kate to be his friend. His friend with benefits. Marital benefits, that was.

The days passed quickly for Kate, the nights not so much. Kissing Jared had been a mistake because all she could think about was…kissing him again.

She lay in her bed. Three o'clock in the morning. She should be fast asleep, not wide-awake, but thinking about Jared sleeping down the hall in his underwear or maybe nothing else wasn't helping. She kept waiting for Cassidy—

The baby.

Kate bolted upright. Cassidy hadn't woken up tonight. That wasn't normal.

Her heart pounding, Kate hurried to the baby's room. The door was ajar. She peeked inside.

Cassidy lay with her hands behind her head sound asleep. Her tiny chest rose with her even breaths. So small, so perfect.

Even when Cassidy fussed or cried.

Kate's heart rate returned to normal, but love for the child welled up inside of her. She'd finally found what had eluded her all these years—unconditional love. Kate thought it wasn't possible for anyone to love her no matter what she said or did.

But Cassidy did.

Thank you, Susan. Thank you so very much.

As Kate watched the baby sleep, she sensed a presence behind, Jared. Could he ever love her the way the baby did? Without reserve. Without conditions. Totally. Completely.

Forever.

She backed out of the room and closed the door so only a small crack remained.

"I heard you get up," he said.

Dark razor stubble covered his face. His tousled hair and sleep rumpled T-shirt and boxer briefs made him look sexy. A tad dangerous. Her pulse quickened.

Forget cardio exercise. Between Cassidy and Jared, Kate's heart got enough of a workout.

"Sorry," she said. "I was worried about Cassidy."

He took a step toward the baby's room. "Is something wrong?"

His concern made him even more attractive. He adored Cassidy, and had jumped into his new role as stay-at-home dad without looking back. Kate respected that, respected him.

"She didn't wake up tonight," Kate said. "I wanted to make sure she was okay."

He straightened. "And?"

"She's fine. Sound asleep. The way she should be."

"Good."

He looked good. She thought about her big, empty bed. But that was only loneliness talking. And attraction. Two things she couldn't allow to get in the way and complicate matters.

"We may have turned a corner," he said.

A knot formed in her throat. "Corner?"

"Cassidy sleeping through the night."

"That would be great."

Except he would be free to go home. The baby had adjusted to her nap schedule at home and no longer threw tantrums at bedtime. A part of Kate hoped tonight was an anomaly. She wasn't ready to say goodbye to Jared.

"You'd better get some sleep," he said. "Don't you have a big meeting tomorrow?"

She always had a big meeting, but she appreciated Jared remembering. If only he'd sweep her off her feet and carry her to bed the way he used to. "I do have a meeting."

"I'll take care of Cassidy if she wakes up."

"Thanks."

Kate trudged her way back to her bedroom, making sure she didn't look back because if she had and still saw Jared standing there and watching her, she wouldn't be able to close the door.

She stepped into her room, shut the door and clicked the lock in place.

What was she going to do? Jared made life so much better. His handling the house and the baby helped, but his being here to lend a hand or an ear made such a difference. They ate dinner together, shared their days and helped each other with the chores around the house. They'd become partners, teammates, parents. Kate didn't know how she would get along without him.

And that was a problem.

The problem.

They were playing house. She got that part.

But being "mom" when she was used to having great sex with "dad" who walked around the house in a T-shirt and underwear looking better than your typical Abercrombie & Fitch model wasn't that much fun. Or easy to do. Especially when the lines between playing and real life kept blurring.

Having Jared here, having him help with Cassidy was wonderful. But, Kate realized, it wasn't enough.

It would never be enough.

Jared pushed Cassidy in her stroller along the waterfront path in downtown Portland. His sisters, Heather and Hannah, pushed strollers alongside him.

"How are things going?" Heather asked.

"Good," he said. "It's going well with Cassidy."

"So any change in your arrangement with Kate?" Hannah asked, with a suggestive lift of her eyebrows.

Not the kind of change she meant. "Not as much as I was hoping for."

"And what were you hoping for?" Heather asked. "That she'd show up in your bed naked and attack you?"

"Pretty much."

His sisters laughed.

But it wasn't only about sex or the lack of it. Somewhere between caring for Cassidy and living together as a family, he and Kate had become a team, a parental unit, a couple. The bond between them grew stronger every day. Jared didn't want to lose that when he went back to Seattle.

"She's my wife," he said. "It shouldn't be this difficult."

Hannah sighed: "You've never had a conventional marriage, little brother."

"And Kate did file for divorce," Heather said. "It's not going to be an easy road ahead."

"I'm not giving up," he said.

"Have you thought about what will happen if everything you're doing, all the sacrifices you're making don't change things?" Heather asked.

"No." He glanced at a ship sailing on the Willamette River. "Losing isn't an option. I'm going to make my marriage work no matter what."

He would do whatever it took. He would not fail.

Kate was going to fall in love with him again.

It was just a matter of time.

Unfortunately his boss had called and wanted him back. On Monday. That only gave him three more days to make it happen.

Friday morning, the alarm clock blared. Eyes closed, Kate pounded the top of her nightstand until she hit the snooze button. Good. She wanted to sleep. And then she remembered. Her morning staff meeting. Kate glanced at the clock.

Oh, no. Late.

She must have hit the Snooze a couple of times before this. She threw off the covers, scrambled off the bed and ran to the bathroom. Turning on the shower, she noticed all the towels were gone. Oh. She was supposed to fold the clothes in the dryer last night.

Kate hurried to the laundry room, dug a towel from the dryer and was halfway up the stairs when she bumped into Jared coming down them. She sucked in a breath.

No man should look this good so early. He wore a pair of shorts. And nothing else. She swallowed. Hard.

"Good morning," he said with a smile. "In a hurry?"

Was she? Kate couldn't see past his sweat-drenched chest and his tight abs. Her dry throat could teach the Sahara desert a thing or two. "Uh-huh."

"What are you doing down here?" he asked.

The sweat on his skin gleamed. Her temperature inched up.

"Kate?"

She showed him the towel, trying to concentrate on the damp tendrils framing his face so her gaze wouldn't drift downward.

"I need one, too," he said.

She needed to see whether he'd chosen to wear boxer briefs under his shorts this morning or old-fashioned boxers. Not that knowing mattered. Much. "Dryer. The towels are in the dryer. I forgot to fold the laundry."

"I'll fold it this morning."

His good looks, his rich voice and his glistening skin wreaked havoc with her senses. She didn't like that. "It's my turn."

"I don't mind."

But she did. "I want to do…fold the laundry."

No, what Kate really wanted to do was him. Forget the rules. Forget any more friendly kisses. She gulped.

His gaze raked over her, reminding her she was wearing only a T-shirt. And a pretty short one at that. Her cheeks warmed. She tugged on the hemline.

"Don't do that." His voice sent a ripple of awareness through her. "Your curves are coming back. I like it."

And she liked him. A singsong rhyme from her school-days played in her head. Kate and Jared sitting in a tree K-I-S-S-I-N-G. Forget the tree. The stairs would work fine.

Oh, boy, she had to get a grip. Or take a spin on the dryer's cool down cycle.

Remember the rules. Set boundaries. Keep her distance.

So what if he had an amazing body? And looked hot after finishing a rep of crunchies or push-ups or whatever he did to keep himself looking so great. He was still just a guy. Man. Dad.

Who was leaving for Seattle on Sunday.

She clutched the towel.

Unless she wanted to hand him her heart with a Fragile Do Not Break sticker attached, she had to stop ogling him like a new pair of shoes from Nordstrom. "I need a shower."

"Me, too." The invitation in his eyes sent her heart slamming against her chest, and she struggled to breathe. "Want to join me?"

Yes. No. What if the baby woke up? "No, thanks. I'm running late."

"You can go first, Katie."

"Thanks." But she wasn't so sure he was doing her any favors.

He walked past her, brushing his shoulder against her bare arm. Accidental or on purpose, she didn't know, but heat exploded at the point of contact. The attraction between them had grown. Bad. Very bad.

"And Kate," he called.

She glanced back.

"Make sure you leave me some hot water."

That wasn't going to be a problem. The coldest setting was probably going to be too warm for her. "Don't worry," she said. "You'll have plenty."

She wanted him. Thanks to their early morning encounter on the stairs, Jared knew it. He'd won.

Won.

He was going to talk to Kate about making this marriage of convenience more convenient and real. Tonight. He wanted his wife—body, heart and soul.

His cell phone rang. He recognized his lawyer's number on the display. "Hello."

But as his attorney updated him, Jared's hope and conviction died. His day had been great up to this point, but now...

He snapped his phone shut in a state of shock that failed to block his rising anger. Or his hurt.

Kate didn't want him. She never had.

He scooped a crying Cassidy from her crib and prepared her bottle with jerky efficiency.

When he heard Kate's car in the driveway a few minutes later, he stalked to the door to meet her.

"Hello," Kate said with a smile. She kissed the baby's cheek, then his. "How was your day?"

The collar of his shirt tightened around his neck. "My day was going fine until I got a phone call from my lawyer telling me the judge signed the judgment of dissolution of our marriage."

"Oh, no." The color drained from Kate's face. She covered her gaping mouth with her hands. "I'm so sorry. I never told my attorney to stop the divorce proceedings."

Her obvious shock reassured him. A little. "Did you forget—?"

"Of course I forgot." She glared at him. "Do you think I would do this on purpose?"

And chance losing Cassidy? Hell, no. But the betrayal, intentional or not, cut deeply. Letting it go wasn't so easy. "Probably not."

"Definitely not." Kate might have changed and softened some of her edges, but she still had a spine. She looked him squarely in the eyes. "Between Cassidy, work and you showing up, I've been a little busy. I agreed to the arrangement and I'm sticking to that. No matter what."

The sincerity in her voice removed what doubt remained. His anger dissipated. "I believe you."

Her gaze held his for a moment. The connection between them was still there, though dimmed by a fog of distrust and hurt.

"So what happens now?" she asked.

"There is a thirty-day waiting period until the dissolution is final," he explained, having memorized his lawyer's words. "If we want to stay together and give notice to the court, our marriage will continue as if we never filed for divorce."

Kate picked up the telephone. "Let's call now."

Her eagerness pleased Jared, but not even Kate's determination would be able to turn back the clock. "It's after five. The courts are closed until Monday."

She put the phone back in place and looked up at him, her eyes anxious. "You'll be in Seattle on Monday."

Kate sounded so sad, looked so lost.

"It'll be okay." But Jared's words did nothing to remove the heaviness centered in his chest. "We're in this together, remember?"

But suddenly that didn't seem nearly enough.

CHAPTER TEN

"I CAN'T believe it's time for me to go," Jared said as he opened his suitcase. Especially when he'd wanted to go home with his family in tow.

Sitting crisscross on the guest room floor, Kate folded his clothes. "The time's gone so fast."

He was glad she thought so, too.

Jared glanced around the small room. "I wish I could pack the entire house and bring it with me to Seattle."

"I thought you had a two-bedroom apartment."

"I'd make it fit," he said. "I'd do anything to have us be together."

"We'll be together on weekends."

"And that's enough for you?"

She stuck out her chin. "It has to be."

"Does it?" he pressed, knowing tomorrow he didn't want to say goodbye to her for one day let alone five.

"Yes, it does." She looked away. "Please don't make this any harder than it has to be."

The emotion in her voice gave him hope. "I don't want this to be hard on us. I just want us to be together."

"Me, too." Kate folded a T-shirt with the same competence she did everything else and handed the neat, white square to him. "Make sure you leave some clothes here so you won't have to pack an extra bag when you come down on weekends."

"You're so practical, Kate." He'd always respected that about her, but her practicality was getting in the way of what he wanted, what was best for her, him and Cassidy. Jared placed the T-shirt on top of his shorts.

"I have to be, to take care of Cassidy."

"It won't be easy for you." And that bothered him. Eating regular meals had helped her put on weight. Sleeping through the night had gotten rid of the dark circles under her eyes. She looked healthier and rested. He didn't want her to fall back into the old routine of neglecting herself when things got hectic. "I hate leaving you."

"I hate to see you go." She smiled ruefully. "It's been great having you here. I'll be the first to admit I have no idea how I'll get along without you."

"So come with me."

"To Seattle?"

"Yes."

For a second, he saw the idea take hold in her eyes and then her familiar caution, her damn practicality, returned. "You mean next weekend?"

"I mean for good." He tossed a pair of pants in his suitcase, not caring if they were folded or not. "I don't want us to be apart."

"I'd love if we could be together, but this isn't only about us."

"Being together would be good for Cassidy."

"I meant my firm," Kate corrected, her voice strong and determined. "Don't forget, twenty people rely on me for their livelihood. The potential for growth is phenomenal. It makes financial sense for me to stay here and guide the company through this period and ensure our family's future."

Financial sense, sure. But with his suitcase half-packed and facing a week of late night telephone calls from a hotel room, Jared wasn't feeling sensible. He'd even keep the no-sex rule in place if it meant having her with him.

"Emily Butler could run the firm for a while," he said. "She seems sharp with a lot of savvy."

"She is and a dedicated worker. But she's also pregnant and will be taking maternity leave this summer," Kate explained.

"There has to be someone else."

"It's my company. My name on the placard."

"You're my wife and Cassidy's mother."

"That's not fair." Kate frowned. "I shouldn't have to choose."

He thought about Brady and Susan. "Sometimes life isn't fair, Kate."

"I want to be your wife and Cassidy's mom, but you're asking me to give up—" Kate took a breath and exhaled slowly "—my home, my career, my life. Everything I've worked for and dreamed of since I was young."

He sympathized with her, but too much was riding on this to let it go. Weren't his dreams as important as hers? Wasn't their family?

He needed to play to win. Even if it was dirty. The means justified the ends, as his father always said.

"Isn't having a family part of your dream?" he asked.

"You know it is."

"So how can you walk away from our family? From us?"

"I'm not walking away from anything." She crossed her arms over her chest. "I don't want to fight."

"We need to discuss this."

"The last time we discussed this we ended up in divorce court." Her eyes pleaded with him. "It's too soon for me to make the kind of decision you want."

"It's been two weeks."

"Two wonderful weeks," she admitted. "And that's part of the problem. We shouldn't make a decision when our judgment is clouded."

"My mind is made up. I want you, Kate. I want you and Cassidy in my life."

"We are in your life."

"But not where I want you." He took her hands in his. "We could have a real marriage if you moved to Seattle with me."

"We could still have a real marriage if I didn't."

"Is that what you want?" he asked, tension charging the air. "A real marriage?"

He'd offered her a real marriage. A real family. Kate had wanted both, more than anything, but she didn't want to accept his terms.

She spent a restless night in her big, empty bed thinking and dreaming about Jared. Kate missed him so much. And he wasn't even gone yet.

"Happy Mother's Day."

Pathetic. He was leaving, and all she could do was dream about him complete with realistic audio. She needed to gain control over her emotions.

The mattress depressed.

She opened her eyes and saw Jared sitting next to her

with Cassidy in his arms. He'd ditched his everyday T-shirt and shorts for a black polo shirt and khaki slacks. The smart casual look suited him well, as did the way his damp hair curled at the ends. She fought the urge to reach out and touch his smooth, recently shaved face.

He looked good, so mouthwatering good.

Kate wondered if she was still dreaming. She propped herself up on her elbows. Nope. She was awake. "About last night."

He smiled, those dimples of his appearing with a vengeance, and she felt sucker punched. "Not now."

But they hadn't come to any conclusion, decision. And he was leaving. Tonight.

He watched her with an odd expression in his eyes and motioned toward the other side of the bed. A pink smoothie, a chocolate doughnut, a white envelope, a blue box and a single red rose sat on a tray.

Wow. Kate sat up. "What's going on?"

"It's for you."

Presents. After they'd fought. That didn't make any sense. Confused, she looked at him.

"Happy Mother's Day," he said.

Cassidy giggled and waved her hands.

Mother's Day. Kate was a mother.

A swell of emotion swept through her. Tears stung her eyes. She hadn't expected this. She'd never thought of today being anything other than the day Jared went back to Seattle.

"Did you think I would forget?" he asked.

Not trusting her voice, she shook her head. "I forgot."

"You've been busy."

"It's not that," she admitted, feeling overwhelmed by and unworthy of the attention. "I spent so many years celebrating this day with different mothers, but never my mother. I know today is a big deal for your family, but the holiday never seemed important to me."

"Today is the start of a new tradition then," he said.

Their first family tradition. She stared at a grinning Cassidy. Kate wiped the drool from the baby's chin with the sleeve of her nightshirt.

"Koo," the baby said.

She felt a sudden squeezing pain. "This should be Susan's day."

"Susan would be proud of you. She would appreciate everything you do for Cassidy." Jared traced Kate's jawline with his fingertip. "The way I do."

"Thank you so much for everything." Kate sniffled. "You don't know what this means to me."

She kissed Cassidy's cheek. She went to kiss Jared's cheek, but he turned so she kissed him on the lips instead. Warm and nice, his kiss tasted like a mix of coffee and chocolate doughnuts.

Jared grinned. "Gotcha."

He did. He had her. All of her.

The realization left her speechless and more than a little scared. She didn't want him to leave tonight, but she couldn't go with him, either.

He reached over her and picked up a rectangular navy-blue box patterned like the strips on a grosgrain ribbon. "This is for you."

She untied the navy and white ribbon imprinted with the name Aaron Basha and removed the lid. Inside laid a silver—no, white gold—charm bracelet and the prettiest pink enamel baby shoe charm with a diamond strap and diamond hearts on the toe. "I love it."

"Let me put the bracelet on you." He clasped the chain around her wrist.

"This was so thoughtful of you." She stared at the dangling charm. "Thank you."

He handed her the white envelope. "Now this."

Kate pulled out a lovely card with a little girl walking through a field of purple irises and green grass. The printed sentiment brought a lump to her throat, but the handwritten words at the bottom made her heart skip a beat. Okay, three. She reread them again.

You are my wife and my life. Whether I'm here or in Seattle that won't change. Forget the rules. I want a real marriage with you. I want us to be a real family. All you have to do is say the word.

Love,
Jared (& Cassidy, too!)

Kate stared into his eyes. She knew the risks, but she was willing to take the chance. She wanted a real marriage. She wanted them to be a real family.

Long distance didn't matter. The marriage would work.

She cleared her throat. "Yes."

A nerve twitched at his neck. "Yes?"

"Isn't that the word I'm supposed to say?"

A smile erupted on his face, not only with dimples but lines crinkling the corner of his eyes. He gathered her up in his arm.

Jared looked down at her with such tender affection she thought her heart might burst with happiness. He lowered his mouth to hers.

The moment his lips touched her, emotion burst through Kate with the force of a rocket launcher. She could no longer pretend she didn't feel anything, no longer hold back all her feelings for Jared, all her longings.

He pressed his lips against hers. The warm taste filled her up, but she didn't think she could ever get enough of him. This was what she'd been missing, what she needed. And Kate never wanted the kiss to end.

Heat emanated deep within her, sparking a need she knew could not be filled. At least not with the baby here. Kate could tell by the way Jared held back, not touching her, that he was conscious of the baby's presence, too.

They were a family, and sometimes that meant having to wait even if you didn't want to.

"Ah-gah, gah."

Jared slowly drew the kiss to an end. "I think Cassidy is getting bored."

That was the least boring kiss ever. Kate's mouth felt bruised and utterly loved. She inhaled to calm her rapid pulse and fill her lungs with much needed air. "Um, Jared, that wasn't a friendly kiss."

Mischief gleamed in his eyes. "Now that we're husband and wife for real and not in name only, the marital kiss takes precedence over the friend kiss."

"I can live with that."

"I thought so."

Cassidy squealed with delight.

"Group hug," Jared said. "Or should I say, family hug."

"We're a family, Cassidy," Kate said. "A real family."

He smiled. "I like the sound of that."

"You know what I'd really like right now?" she asked.

"Me, too." He glanced at the clock. "But it's too early to put Cassidy down for her nap."

"I hate to burst your bubble but this—" Kate patted the mattress "—isn't what I was talking about?"

Lines creased his forehead. "What do you want?"

"Breakfast." She grinned mischievously. "That doughnut sure smells yummy."

"I'm supposed to be the yummy one." Looking at Cassidy, he sighed. "Your mommy has the wrong thing on her mind this morning."

"No, she's just more practical about our other commitments like meeting your family at church in an hour," Kate said.

"You're no fun," Jared complained.

"Wait until we get home," she promised. "I'll show you how fun I can be."

He raised a brow. "What do you have in mind?"

"I thought maybe you could give me one final present for Mother's Day."

"What's that?"

She met his gaze directly. "You."

He sucked in a breath. "Should I wear a bow?"

"Please do," she said in her huskiest voice. "And nothing else."

"That baby gets cuter every time I see her." Staring at Cassidy sitting on Kate's lap, Frank flipped the steaks and hamburgers cooking on the grill in the backyard. Every Mother's Day under the shady canopy of the towering Douglas firs and the blossoming cherry trees, he threw a barbecue for his wife, daughters and daughters-in-law.

One of the many Reed family traditions. "Kate looks good. Not so skinny and pale."

Jared nodded. She looked radiant, her face glowing.

"So you're heading back to Seattle tonight?" Frank asked.

"Yes." But Jared wasn't thinking that far ahead. He only wanted to get home. Speaking of which, he needed to swipe a bow from the pile of presents on the picnic table. "I'll be back on Friday."

Sooner if he got the opportunity.

"So you think this long distance arrangement will work out?" Frank asked.

"Yes," Jared said, tired of rehashing the details with every single member of his family, as if they knew more about the situation than he did. "Kate and I are going to make this marriage work."

"Your mother mentioned the official dissolution being signed by the judge."

"Seems like Mom told everybody." Jared took a sip of his iced tea. "We're going to take care of that tomorrow."

Frank peppered the meat. "What if you used the threat of divorce to force Kate to move to Seattle instead?"

Bitterness coated Jared's mouth. "Funny, but you're not the first person to tell me that today."

His siblings had suggested a similar idea. His father must have been the ringleader.

Frank adjusted the heat on the gas grill. "So…"

"I can't do that to Kate, Dad."

"Can't or won't?" his father asked. "Sometimes a man has to do things he'd rather not, but the means justify the end, son. Kate will thank you for this later."

Jared looked across the grass at Kate tossing a ball in the air. "She'd hate me. And she'd have every right."

"You've been watching too many of those daytime talk shows while you've been home." Frank laughed. "You're going soft."

Not soft, Jared thought. Just a bit more evolved. He shook his empty glass. "I need a refill."

His father nodded. "Think about what I said."

"I don't have to think about it, Dad. I won't do that to her. To us."

"Somebody has to do something," Frank muttered.

Jared hoped his father cooled down. But after lunch, as his mother and sisters cleared away the litter of wrapping paper and dirty dishes, Frank approached Kate.

"You ought to be going with him," his father said.

Kate held the baby a little tighter. "I'm sorry, Frank. We feel this arrangement is better for us right now."

"It's not good for Jared."

"Dad, that's enough," Jared said sharply.

Frank ignored him. "The judge signed the paperwork. Jared would have every right to go through with the divorce if you won't go with him to Seattle."

Kate drew in a breath, her stricken eyes seeking Jared's. "Would you do that?"

"No." He'd never understood her concerns about his family's intrusiveness, but he did now. And it was time to put an end to it. "You guys know I love you, and put up with the nosiness and all your advice, but today a few of you Reeds went a little too far suggesting I do what Dad just told Kate I should do and that's...wrong."

"You all should be ashamed of yourselves," Margery announced, rushing to Kate's side like a bear protecting her cub. "I apologize for all my misguided children. Especially the old one who should know better."

A red-faced Frank mumbled an apology.

"We wanted to help," Sam said.

Hannah nodded. So did Tucker. And Heather.

Jared listened to his family one by one justify their reasons. He'd always considered family, family. Extended, immediate, distant. It hadn't mattered. Until today. He still loved each one of them, but he had his own family now and they needed to come first.

"I'm not the one you should be apologizing to." Jared stared at his father and four siblings. "I know you want to help. That's what we do for each other. Help. But think about what you asked me to do. The end does not always justify the means. Especially if it hurts the one person who means the most to me. My wife."

Jared hated making a scene, but his family had left him no choice. He put his arm around Kate and the baby. "It's time to go home."

On the drive home, Kate dabbed tears from the corner of her eyes. She thought she'd respected and loved Jared before, but those feelings couldn't compare to how she felt about him now.

She was used to handling everything and making a place for herself. She needed to do that on her own in order to avoid being disappointed. It was easier that way. Safer. But today Jared had taken on his father, his family, for her. Without any prompting. Without being asked.

Her astonished heart overflowed with joy. "I can't believe you said those things."

He glanced sideways at her. "I'm sorry it had to come to that."

She heard the regret in his voice, but the sincerity filled her with warmth. She was no longer alone. "I'm not."

"You're not?"

"Nope." Kate smiled. She would not take his championing her for granted. She would prove herself worthy of his support. "No one has ever stood up for me like you did. You made feel good. Special. Thank you."

"I only did what needed to be done." Jared covered her hand with his. "I should have spoken up earlier, but I didn't realize…"

Staring at their linked fingers, at the pink baby shoe charm on the new bracelet around her wrist, she felt everything she needed dangling at her fingertips. If only she could reach out and grasp it. If only she could prove herself worthy of his love the way he had just proved himself deserving of hers.

Kate knew she could make their marriage work. She loved him. No doubt. She wanted to with him. No question.

Jared's actions today showed her he hadn't abandoned her by moving to Seattle without her. Instead of dealing with the troubles in their marriage, he'd listened to his family. He could have done the same thing today, but he hadn't. He'd defended her. He'd changed.

She felt renewed, alive, loved. She didn't want that to end. "So what you said about moving to Seattle…"

He squeezed her hand. "I'm not going to force you to move."

Kate drew strength from his touch. She could feel the love flowing from him, and she knew it was her turn to give that feeling back to him. "But that's what you want."

"I want us to be together," he said.

"I want that, too."

Before she'd tried to control Jared because she'd had so little control of her own life. But now they were a couple, a family, and she couldn't continue to operate the same way. Family made sacrifices for each other. If she wanted to keep their family together, to make their marriage work, Kate would have to prove herself worthy of his love.

She took a deep breath. "What if Cassidy and I moved to Seattle, and I tried telecommuting? I'd still have to travel some, but I could set up a satellite office."

Jared pulled into the driveway and turned off the car. "You would do that?"

"I'm willing to try to see if it works," she said. "If it does, we can talk about what the next step would be."

Like the house. Her firm. So many things. "But I'll need to find child care. I know I can't work while taking care of Cassidy at the same time."

"No problem. We can hire a nanny or use a day care." He sounded pleased, happy. "Are you sure about this, Katie?"

She had the family she'd dreamed about. A husband who'd stood up to his family in her defense. A daughter who loved her no matter what. Kate wasn't about to risk that. She would do whatever having a real marriage and keeping her family together took. She would be the perfect wife and mother. And businesswoman, too. She could do it. She would do it. "Yes, I'm sure."

Jared opened his car door. "Stay here."

"Why?"

He removed a sleeping Cassidy from her car seat and

grabbed the diaper bag. "Give me five minutes. That's all I ask."

"Okay." Kate would use the time to formulate a plan on how her move to Seattle would work and telecommuting and child care...

Four minutes later, a text message appeared on her BlackBerry: Go upstairs.

Kate did. All the doors were closed except the one to her bedroom. She stepped inside. "Jared?"

"Are you ready?" he called from the bathroom.

"For what?"

He walked out wearing nothing but a red bow. "To unwrap your present."

CHAPTER ELEVEN

JARED had won. He'd gotten exactly what he wanted. Kate and Cassidy had been living in his apartment for the past two weeks. So how come victory felt so hollow?

He stared out the window of his hotel room on San Francisco's Union Square. His meeting with the CEO had gone well. Tomorrow he would tour the manufacturing facilities; the next day he had more meetings and the day after that...

He hoped to finish in the morning so he could catch an earlier flight home.

Home.

Jared had only been home for five days since Kate and Cassidy arrived in Seattle. Unfortunately the move hadn't solved the problem of their spending more time together. Granted, he would see them less if he had to add a weekly commute to Portland, but was the limited time together worth disrupting their lives?

He'd tried to think of a solution, but his consulting job required constant travel, often weeks away at a time, visiting companies his clients wanted to invest in. What could he do? He loved his job, except...

He had so much more in his life to go home to now.

Jared stepped away from the window and sat on the bed. Numbers needed to be crunched and research completed, but he didn't open his laptop. Instead he grabbed his cell phone and hit the number three on his keypad.

On the fourth ring, he heard a "hello" that sounded better than the song of a heavenly choir. Okay, he was exaggerating, but only slightly.

"Hey, gorgeous," he said.

"Jared? Hang on a minute."

Silence filled the receiver while he felt a twinge of disappointment. He wanted to hear Kate's voice, not wait and wonder what she was doing without him.

"I'm back," she said less than thirty seconds later.

"You sound surprised to hear from me," he said. "Who else would be calling you at this hour?"

"I don't know," she teased. "Maybe a tall, dark and handsome stranger."

"Well, I'm not a stranger."

Though he worried with all the time he spent on the road, Cassidy would forget who he was.

"You're not very modest, either." She sounded like she was smiling.

"So how are my two girls?" he asked.

"Cassidy's been a little fussy," Kate admitted. "Her first tooth came in."

"Yeah?" He sunk back into a king-size down pillow. "Sorry I missed that."

"There will be other teeth," Kate said, trying to reassure him.

It didn't work.

"Other teeth aren't the same as the first one." Jared wondered what milestones he might miss. Cassidy's first step, her first word, her first boyfriend.

"I can e-mail you a picture."

His dissatisfaction grew. "I don't want to watch Cassidy grow up on a computer screen."

Silence. "Well, I could always send the pictures to your cell phone."

Her lightness sounded forced.

"Are you getting any sleep?" he asked, instantly concerned and wishing he could see her face.

"Cassidy's still sticking to her schedule," Kate said, not exactly answering his question.

He'd try a different tactic. "How's work?"

"Heating up a bit."

"Trouble?"

"beBuzz has turned into a bigger project than we'd anticipated."

Her strained voice bothered him. "Are you okay?"

"A little tired, but I'm okay." As she spoke, he heard a muffled sound in the background. "How about you? Are you okay?"

"I'll be better when I'm back home with you and the baby." He had memorized his itinerary. "Only three more days."

Silence greeted him.

"Kate?"

"Sorry," she said absently. "I thought I heard the baby."

She sounded distracted. She must be worried about Cassidy. He should let her go.

"I'm going to do a little work before bed."

"Me, too," she said. "Good—"

"Wait." Jared wasn't ready to say goodbye. "I miss you, Kate. I really miss you and Cassidy."

"I miss you, too," Kate said. "A lot."

"I'll call tomorrow." He hated to hang up, but the longer he stayed on the phone the later she would have to stay up to finish her work. She sounded tired despite her denial that Cassidy had gotten off her schedule. "Bye."

He disconnected the line. The phone call hadn't helped fill the void inside him. He sat in lonely silence, thinking about her voice and her words.

I miss you, too. A lot.

She wanted him home; he wanted to be home.

Three more days. Less than seventy-two hours until he saw her again. Jared could make it. He had no other choice.

Kate stared at the receiver in her hand. Her heart ached. She missed Jared so much more than she ever thought possible. If only he were here now…

But he wasn't and wouldn't be. Kate had moved to Seattle, but he was still gone all the time. She'd known that would be the case. Still… She sighed.

At least she got to see Cassidy's new tooth.

Kate returned to the small apartment kitchen that had been turned into a satellite office for her public relations firm. Two of her employees worked at the table covered with laptops and paper and speakerphone. Next to them on the floor, Cassidy sat in her lilac Bumbo baby seat.

Kate smiled at the baby. "That was your daddy. He misses us."

Us.

The word warmed her heart. That counted for something.

Sean Owens, her twenty-something assistant and the crush of all the unmarried females in the office, adjusted his black-rimmed glasses. "Is Jared coming home?"

"He'll be back as soon as he can." Kate didn't like her employees knowing about her personal life, but in this case she'd had no choice. "Friday at the latest."

Maisie McFall, a thirty-something writer with short, spiky black hair and four years nanny experience, looked up from her laptop. "If you were in Portland, this situation would be a lot easier to manage."

Her words echoed Kate's own doubts. If she were back in Portland, her life would be easier and back to normal, too. She stared at the charm bracelet around her wrist.

"I told Jared I'd give Seattle a go," she said. He'd proven his love. It was her turn. "I have to do that."

And she would. She had to.

Kate understood what was at stake. She needed to make sure they remained together because she was the only one who knew what the lack of a family could do, not just to her and Jared, but Cassidy. Kate had spent her entire childhood trying and failing to fit in, to be a part of other people's families. She wasn't going to fail with her own family.

Sean refilled her coffee cup. "If this situation with beBuzz gets any worse…"

Her newest client was facing an onslaught of bad press. Accusations their latest financial report had been misrepresented had resulted in the "resignation" of the CEO and CFO, and a downward spiral of the once highly touted stock. If the negative publicity and hints of criminal activity continued, the once successful company could face bankruptcy. Or worse.

"I know what's at stake." Not only for her client, but for her own firm. "I appreciate you coming up here today. Between you and the team in office we'll get this done."

Another all-nighter, do doubt. The second in a row for Kate, but she hadn't told Jared. Why worry him when there was nothing he could do from so far away?

Cassidy yawned.

"I'm going to put the baby to bed and I'll be right back." As Kate picked up the baby from the Bumbo, Cassidy puckered. "Don't get that look on your face. It's bedtime. Be a good girl and go to sleep."

Cassidy pouted, her lower lip quivering.

Kate kissed the baby's cheek. Hot. "Oh, no."

"What is it?" Maisie asked, already on her feet.

"Cassidy's burning up." Kate touched the baby's forehead. "I'm sure she has a fever."

"Have you run over the schedule for the new CEO's interview on CNBC?" Kate asked two days later, holding Cassidy. Antibiotics had helped the baby's ear infection, but she was completely off-schedule and so was Kate. If not for caffeine, she'd be flat on her back comatose.

You're the one who's incredible, Kate. I'm amazed at how much you've done with Cassidy. You can handle anything.

Kate hadn't told Jared about the ear infection, about the problems with beBuzz or pulling all-nighters. He believed she could handle anything. And she didn't want to disappoint him.

She heard murmuring on the other end of the speakerphone and massaged one of her aching temples.

Sean hit Mute. "This isn't looking good."

"Have faith." At this point that was all they had left. Cassidy whimpered. Frustrated, Kate sighed. She needed to take her own advice and have faith herself. "Are you hungry, baby?"

"I'll take her." Maisie stood. "Cassidy and I have an understanding when it comes to eating. The messier, the better. Isn't that right, baby?"

"Thanks." Guilt mixed with gratitude. Kate owed both employees for going above and beyond with beBuzz and Cassidy. Jared would be back tomorrow and by then, she hoped things would have settled down both on the home and work fronts.

"Look at this, Kate," Sean said.

As Maisie strapped the baby into the high chair, Kate sat at the table and stared at the chart on Sean's laptop. beBuzz's stock had risen eight percent since the market opened two hours ago. A good sign after a fifty-seven percent drop since Monday. "The damage control is working."

Sean nodded. "You're the spin master."

Kate wouldn't disagree. The room *was* sort of spinning.

She rubbed her forehead and glanced at the baby eating her rice cereal. White mush seemed to be everywhere but inside Cassidy's mouth. "We're not out of the woods yet."

Maisie wiped the baby's face with a...dish towel. Were they out of washcloths and napkins?

"Okay," Emily Butler, second in command, said finally. "We have the schedule and I will be accompanying Mr. Leclerc to the studio for his interview and the press conference."

Kate hit the speaker button. "Sounds good. The stock

is up slightly, but we have a long way to go. We need an all-out blitz today."

As she stood, the chart on the screen blurred. Kate blinked and refocused. Lack of sleep was catching up with her. She headed to the overused, but well-appreciated coffeepot.

Reaching for a cup in the upper cabinet, she felt woozy. Shaky. Something crashed on the counter.

"Kate?" a voice asked from behind her.

Her legs wobbled. She reached for the counter.

I'm sorry, Jared. I failed you.

And saw...

Black.

Jared entered the hospital with only Kate on his mind. He hadn't been able to stop thinking and worrying about her since he received the call five excruciating hours ago. An older woman with blue-gray hair and a pink smock directed him to a waiting area where he found Sean, a woman named Maisie and Cassidy, in her stroller fast asleep.

The content look on the baby's face brought a momentary relief. At least Cassidy was fine.

"Where's Kate?" Jared asked. "How is she doing?"

"She's with the doctor," Sean explained. "Kate has a concussion. She hit her head when she collapsed."

"How did Kate collapse?" Jared asked, noticing the exchange of glances between his wife's employees.

"Talk to Kate about that," Sean said.

Jared wanted to do just that as soon as he could. "Would you mind watching Cassidy again?"

"I don't mind at all, Mr. Malone," Maisie said, and Jared didn't feel the need to correct her. "She's a great baby and takes her medicine from us without much of a fuss."

"Medicine?" Kate had never mentioned anything about Cassidy needing medication. "For what? Her new tooth?"

"An ear infection," Sean explained.

What was going on? Jared's unease grew. Kate's employees knew more about his daughter than he did. "I'll be in Kate's room if you need me."

Walking down the hospital corridor brought back memories of Boise. Running into Kate at Don's office. Seeing Cassidy for the first time. Saying goodbye to their best friends. But he couldn't concentrate on the past, not when Kate needed him.

Jared went into her room. She lay in the bed, an IV in her left arm, a white bandage on her forehead. Her pale face brought a rush of guilt. Would this have happened if he hadn't been away? A wave of nausea overtook his stomach.

The doctor, a young Indian woman with thick black hair, cleared her throat.

Forcing a smile, Jared put on his game face. "Hey."

"Hi," Kate mumbled, looking dazed. "Cassidy?"

"She's fine. Napping." Jared touched Kate's right hand. She seemed so fragile. "Sean and Maisie are with her in the waiting area. My parents are on the way."

"Okay. Good," Kate said, her voice fading.

The doctor greeted him. "I'm Dr. Pradhan."

"Jared Reed."

"Your wife has suffered a level 3 concussion," the doctor said. "The CT scan showed no skull fracture or bleeding, but we are going to keep her overnight for observation."

"Is it serious?"

"Head injuries, especially with loss of consciousness are always taken seriously, but a concussion is a type of closed head trauma and generally not considered a life-threatening injury. However, there can be short-term and long-term effects."

Not life-threatening. Key point.

"I am concerned about the level of fatigue that caused Kate's collapse in the first place," the doctor said.

"She fell because she was tired?"

Dr. Pradhan checked the chart. "Fainted would be a more accurate term based on the description of what happened."

Jared had wondered whether Kate would take care of herself when he wasn't around, but he never thought she would wind up hospitalized. He didn't understand. She had told him she'd been a little tired, but so was every working mom. She never hinted something was wrong or the baby ill. He scratched his head.

"Cassidy?" Kate asked.

She'd asked the same question before. That couldn't be good. Worried, Jared looked at the doctor.

"Repeating the same thing over and over again is called perseverating and a symptom of a concussion," the doctor explained. "Just answer Kate's question."

"Cassidy's fine." He patted her hand and stared at the charm bracelet around Kate's wrist. "She's in the waiting room with Sean and Maisie."

"Okay," Kate said.

Not okay. Jared hated this. He hated seeing Kate this way. He hated feeling as if he were somewhat to blame. He wanted to know what had happened. He needed to know.

"So what do we do, Doctor?" he asked.

"We wait."

* * *

Oh, boy. She hurt. Her brain felt like leftover oatmeal. Either that or someone had stuffed soggy cotton balls into her head. Kate opened her eyes. The light made her squint.

Hospital. She was in the hospital. And Cassidy...was okay.

Her pounding head and blurry vision made her squeeze her eyes shut. She opened them and blinked. Jared came into focus, his intense gaze resting squarely on her.

He'd come back.

Her heart thumped.

"You're here."

His soft smile practically caressed. "Where else would I be?"

"I—I missed you," she croaked. "Water, please."

As he pushed a button, her bed raised so she was sitting up. Kate felt wobbly. As she adjusted to being upright, Jared poured her a glass of water.

She smelled flowers. Looking past Jared, Kate saw bouquets of all shapes and sizes. She also noticed a box of her favorite chocolates.

He handed her the glass. She drank. The water quenched her thirst and cleared a few of the dust bunnies from her mind. Enough so she remembered.

Reality crashed down on her. Everything she'd done, the perfect image she'd projected for so many years, had collapsed with her.

Over. It was all over. Kate nearly dropped her glass.

Jared took the glass. He sat on the edge of the bed, his thigh pressing against her. "Do you need anything?"

You.

The compassion on his face twisted her insides. Fear and uncertainty rooted themselves in her.

"Where is Cassidy?" Kate asked.

"With my parents," he said. "My entire family is here. Cassidy is getting used to all of them."

The throbbing pain in Kate's head was nothing compared to the ache of her heart. She swallowed a sob. "I'm sorry. If I'd been holding Cassidy when I fainted…"

"But you weren't holding her." His warm, calm voice kept Kate afloat. "She's fine and you're going to be fine."

She wanted to believe him.

Since Cassidy had come into their lives, Jared had given her no reason to doubt him. Kate clung to that. She wanted him to hold her and tell her it was okay. That no matter what, he would love her; that no matter what he would never leave her.

"I don't understand how this happened," Jared said. His hand covered hers. Warm and strong and protective. "We talked every day. You mentioned being tired, but you never told me about Cassidy's ear infection or a big crisis at work. Why didn't you tell me what was going on, Katie?"

Guilt coated her throat. He'd been nothing but a good husband and a wonderful dad. He deserved an answer. She just didn't know what to say. Past hurts gripped hold of her. If she told him the truth, he would know that she couldn't do it all. That she wasn't perfect. That she had failed.

Kate wanted to believe the truth wouldn't matter. He'd proven he cared about her. He'd wanted to save their marriage. But what if Jared was like the other people in her life? People who didn't want her, who didn't love her, who would abandon her?

Did she trust him enough not to leave her?

Because if Jared left, he would take Cassidy with him.

An iron vise clamped around Kate's heart and squeezed hard, but the pain of the thought of losing the two people she loved most in world would be nothing like the real thing.

Fear scraped her bare. Trust him or not, that was the question. She pressed her lips together.

As she pulled her hand from his, he tightened his grasp. "Please, Kate."

His anguished tone cut into her like a knife. A wound would heal, but this… She looked around the room, at everything except him. If she avoided his eyes, maybe she could avoid talking to him.

"Talk to me," Jared said.

Kate wanted to believe in him, but she couldn't stop thinking about the consequences. If she talked to him, she could destroy the family they'd built together.

She stole a glance at him, expecting to see accusation and anger, but the only thing she saw was concern. For her. Emotion clogged her throat.

A muscle flicked at his jaw. As he closed his hand around hers, his forehead creased with worry. "If you can't trust me enough to talk to me, we're…we're never going to make it."

CHAPTER TWELVE

THE truth of Jared's words brought tears to Kate's eyes.
She teetered between self-protection and full disclosure.
Both had their risks, consequences that could change her
life forever. But if she refused to tell him the truth, if she
couldn't trust him with that same truth, what did that say
about their marriage? Their future? She entwined her
fingers with his.

Logically she knew what to do, but her heart wasn't
convinced. Not after years of having to prove herself
worthy of a home, a family, love. Kate gnawed on her
bottom lip.

He scooted closer. "I want to make this work, but you
have to meet me halfway."

"I let you down." As soon as the words tumbled out of
her mouth, she wanted to stop, to walk out on him before
he walked out on her, but her heart...her heart wouldn't
let her. "The day you left for San Francisco we found ourselves in the middle of a media circus due to financial dis-
crepancies in beBuzz's latest financial report."

"You never said a word about this before."

"I thought...I thought I could handle it. Sean and
Maisie came up to help. But Cassidy got sick and there

wasn't as much time during the day so I worked at night. All night."

Jared's brows knotted. "You just had to call me."

"And say what?" Frustration and fear burned in Kate's throat. "Fly home, I really need to be in Portland because my company is falling apart without me?"

"Yes." His voice was strong. Positive. "I would drop everything if you needed me. If I knew what was going on…"

"You have a responsibility to your boss and your clients."

"I have a responsibility to you. You're my wife. I didn't even know something was wrong until I got the call you were in the hospital. I couldn't think straight. I only wanted to get back to you. As soon as I could."

"I didn't plan on this happening. I never wanted you to…"

"To what?"

She swallowed. "To know."

"Why?"

"Because I agreed to move to Seattle." Kate struggled to keep her voice steady. "How could I make our marriage work and keep our family together if I kept running back to Portland whenever something came up at the office?"

"But you said this was a crisis." Jared's jaw tensed. The moment of silence increased the tension between them. Even though he sat next to her, she'd never felt further from him. "If you would have told me how important—"

"I was afraid to tell you."

"Afraid of what?"

You can handle anything.

Kate forced herself to look at Jared. She was either going to destroy her marriage with the truth. Or save it. "I was afraid of disappointing you. I didn't want to lose you again."

"You would never lose me."

"Yes, I would. If you saw I was weak. Vulnerable. Not perfect. You would leave me."

There. The truth was out. But instead of feeling better, Kate felt as if her world was about to crash down on her. Her shoulders sagged.

She stared at his hand linked with hers. "And since I'm none of those things…"

"Those aren't reasons for a person to leave," Jared said. His words made her want to cry.

"But that's what always happened before." Her voice broke. "If I did something they didn't like, they'd send me away."

His lips parted. "Your foster parents? They would send you away?"

She nodded, ashamed. "Not every foster home was like that. There were some good families. Really decent caring people. The one family Susan and I lived with during high school was great. Well, until they had to move out of state our senior year and couldn't take us with them, but we'd been accepted to college and were turning eighteen so it wasn't so bad."

Jared squeezed her hand. "I never knew."

His tenderness gave her courage, enabling her to continue. "Another family talked about adopting me when I was ten. They were really nice, but the father lost his job and the mother got pregnant and… I figured out if I was perfect, everything would be okay. So I tried to be the perfect daughter, the perfect student, the perfect wife."

His eyes softened. "Oh, Katie."

She didn't want his pity. She wanted his love.

"I thought I'd gotten over my past, but then you wanted

to move to Seattle and I didn't and you went anyway and well, history was repeating itself. Unfortunately I wasn't perfect then, and I'm not perfect now." She looked down at the blanket covering her, feeling lost and alone. "I'm sorry I failed you."

Jared stared at his wife, stunned. He wanted to wipe away her fear and sadness. He wanted to make her smile and feel loved. Not for what she did or didn't do, but for who she was.

"You are Ms. Practical. Ms. Take Charge. Ms. Planner Extraordinaire. I admire those traits, but I love Kate, the whole package. I'm sorry now I didn't dig deeper and get to know that whole package better. But we have our whole lives ahead of us to discover each other."

Her wide eyes filled with wonder. "Our whole lives?"

"You're not getting rid of me that easy." His smiled waned. "But I need to tell you something, too."

"You can tell me anything."

Jared hoped so. Years of living with strangers, many who didn't want her or wouldn't love her, had made Kate vulnerable. She might appear tough, opinionated, stubborn, but she wasn't. Those were ways to keep her heart from being broken again. He'd broken her heart anyway. He'd hurt her. They same as the strangers she'd grown up with, but it wouldn't happen again.

Still for them to move forward, they needed to face the past.

"My entire life," Jared said. "I've only been interested in winning. A video game, an argument or our marriage. I didn't care as long as I came out on top.

"I wanted our marriage to work, not for you or me or us, but so we wouldn't be considered a failure." She stared up at him with her emotions so exposed Jared struggled to continue. "That's why I agreed to the marriage of convenience. That's why I took the time off and went to Portland."

"And now?" she asked.

"Now, I owe you an apology," he admitted. "I thought I loved you when I proposed four years ago and we got married. But that is nothing like the love I feel for you now."

The love she needed. The love they both needed.

And Jared finally understood.

"The only thing I want, Katie. The only thing I need is you."

He pulled her on to his lap, mindful of her head injury and IV cord, and brushed his lips across her nape.

"Before I could leave you for a week or more without any problem. I didn't like it, but I figured when our schedules meshed we were meant to be together. Now—" he pushed a strand of hair off her face "—now I want to go to sleep with you by my side and wake up next to you each and every morning."

"In Seattle," she said, sounding resigned.

That was what he wanted, but that wasn't what Kate needed.

Jared had grown up knowing he could fight or argue or tell his family off, and things would be okay. His family gave him security, support and love no matter what. That was something she didn't have, but he could give that to her now.

And Jared would.

Kate shouldn't have made all the sacrifices, uprooting her life and disrupting her career so that they could live together. He should have been the one to do that.

Not because she owned a company that would make her more money or because he was a consultant and had more flexibility to work part-time or a million other things. But because he was more secure than she was. Jared could give Kate what she needed because he loved her. That love was more important than his job or winning or anything else.

"I did," he admitted. "But being in Seattle is not the best thing for us."

"Us?"

"I want us to move back to Portland."

She inhaled sharply. "Your job?"

"My job is taking care of you and Cassidy. That's what I need to do right now," he explained. "Maybe once we're settled I'll look into doing work at home, consulting or something new."

"But your family—"

"You are my family. You and Cassidy."

Her eyes darkened. "I don't want to alienate your parents."

"My parents will be thrilled to have Cassidy closer. And my dad can use his contacts to help me set up a business."

"Really?"

The hope in her voice brought a smile to his face. "Really. But you need to promise me we'll talk to each other. We'll communicate what's going on in our lives and our hearts no matter what. Our needs, our fears, our dreams nothing will be off-limits."

Her smile lit up her face. "I promise."

"And if we get into an argument or disagreement, nothing is going to change anything. I love you, Kate Malone." He embraced her, wishing they could be this close forever. "I will always love you."

"I love you, too."

"I have something for you." Jared pulled a familiar looking navy-blue box from his jacket pocket. "I've been waiting for the perfect time—"

"There is no such thing as perfect."

He laughed. "Then now is as good a time as any."

She untied the blue and white ribbon and opened the top. Inside the box lay a pink heart charm with diamonds and white flowers on it. "The charm is beautiful."

"Like you."

"Thank you." She removed the heart from the box. "I love it. And you."

"My heart will always be with you." He clipped the charm onto her bracelet. "So be careful with it, okay?"

"I'll cherish your heart always." She held her arm with the bracelet to her chest. "And never break it. Deal?"

"Deal."

Jared sealed their bargain with a kiss. He had only meant to brush his lips against hers, but the way Kate raised up to meet him sent his blood roaring through his veins. He couldn't get enough of her. Of her sweetness and her warmth. Need pulsated through him. He wanted her, but not here. Not now. There would be a lifetime of kisses ahead of them so he drew the kiss to an end.

Oh, boy, Kate thought, trying to control her breathing. What a kiss. What a man. Her man.

"I never thought love could ever be like this." The smile on her lips matched the one in her heart. She'd never experienced such happiness. "I'm so glad I was wrong. I thought you were the one for me, but we got married and nothing really changed. We still acted single, living our separate lives during the week and being married on weekends.

"But since Cassidy came into our lives I saw a new side to you." Joy bubbled inside Kate. "And I fell in love with you all over again. Only this time the love was so much deeper, so much stronger than the first time. And I know this is only the beginning."

He lowered his mouth to hers, his lips soft and gentle. His kiss made her feel special, beautiful, alive. She soaked up the essence that made him the man he was. The man who showed her how amazing love could be. His heartbeat thundered against her chest. Kate smiled. Nothing had ever felt so right.

"You've taught me to trust, Jared." His love for her shone in his eyes and sent a warm glow pulsing through her. "Not only you, but my heart. And my heart keeps screaming over and over again, how much I love you."

"I love you, too."

She relished in the pleasure his words brought. "I want to be with you. I want to be married to you. And I think Cassidy needs a brother or sister. Or both."

His dimpled smile reached his eyes. "No argument here. I agree on all counts.

"It's not going to be easy being parents or have a successful marriage. But we will make it work."

"We."

Not I. "Yes, we."

She and Jared were meant to be together as Susan had written in her letter. Their love was strong enough to overcome whatever came their way. Good or bad. They would succeed. For Cassidy, and for each other.

Kate pressed her lips against his. Forget caffeine. This was the only jolt she needed. He pulled her closer. She went eagerly, her mouth moving over his, taking all he had to give. In his arms, she'd found security and strength, peace and happiness, love and a family. She wanted it all; she wanted him. Today. Tomorrow. Forever.

Jared pulled back. "You're wrong about one thing, though."

"What's that?"

"I know something that's perfect."

Her eyes widened. "What?"

"You." He kissed the top of her hand with all the chivalry of a knight from so long ago. "You are perfect for me."

Coming Next Month

#3949 THE SHERIFF'S PREGNANT WIFE Patricia Thayer
Rocky Mountain Brides

Surprise is an understatement for Sheriff Reed Larkin when he finds out his childhood sweetheart has returned home. After all these years Paige Keenan's smile can still make his heart ache. But what's the secret he can see in her whiskey-colored eyes?

#3950 THE PRINCE'S OUTBACK BRIDE Marion Lennox

Prince Max de Gautier travels to the Australian Outback in search of the heir to the throne. But Max finds a feisty woman who is fiercely protective of her adopted children. Although Pippa is wary of this dashing prince, she agrees to spend one month in his royal kingdom.

#3951 THE SECRET LIFE OF LADY GABRIELLA Liz Fielding

Lady Gabriella March is the perfect domestic goddess—but in truth she's simply Ellie March, who uses the beautiful mansion she is house-sitting to inspire her writing. The owner returns, and Ellie discovers that Dr. Benedict Faulkner is the opposite of the aging academic she'd imagined.

#3952 BACK TO MR & MRS Shirley Jump
Makeover Bride & Groom

Cade and Melanie were the high school prom king and queen. Twenty years on, Cade realizes that he let work take over and has lost the one person who lit up his world. Now he is determined to show Melanie he can be the husband she needs…and win back her heart.

#3953 MEMO: MARRY ME? Jennie Adams

Since her accident, and her problems with remembering things, working in an office can sometimes be hard for Lily Kellaway. But with the new boss, Zach Swift, it feels different. And not just because he is seriously gorgeous! Now he has asked her to join him on a business trip.

#3954 HIRED BY THE COWBOY Donna Alward
Western Weddings

Alexis Grayson has always looked after herself. So what if she is alone and pregnant? Gorgeous cowboy Connor Madsen seems determined to take care of her. And he needs something from her, too—a temporary wife! But soon Alexis realizes she wants to be a *real* wife to Connor.

HRCNM0407

REQUEST YOUR FREE BOOKS!
2 FREE NOVELS PLUS 2
FREE GIFTS!

HARLEQUIN ROMANCE®

From the Heart, For the Heart

YES! Please send me 2 FREE Harlequin Romance® novels and my 2 FREE gifts. After receiving them, if I don't wish to receive any more books, I can return the shipping statement marked "cancel." If I don't cancel, I will receive 4 brand-new novels every month and be billed just $3.57 per book in the U.S., or $4.05 per book in Canada, plus 25¢ shipping and handling per book and applicable taxes, if any*. That's a savings of over 15% off the cover price! I understand that accepting the 2 free books and gifts places me under no obligation to buy anything. I can always return a shipment and cancel at any time. Even if I never buy another book from Harlequin, the two free books and gifts are mine to keep forever.

114 HDN EEV7   314 HDN EEWK

Name	(PLEASE PRINT)	
Address		Apt.
City	State/Prov.	Zip/Postal Code

Signature (if under 18, a parent or guardian must sign)

Mail to the **Harlequin Reader Service®**:
IN U.S.A.: P.O. Box 1867, Buffalo, NY 14240-1867
IN CANADA: P.O. Box 609, Fort Erie, Ontario L2A 5X3

Not valid to current Harlequin Romance subscribers.

Want to try two free books from another line?
Call 1-800-873-8635 or visit www.morefreebooks.com.

* Terms and prices subject to change without notice. NY residents add applicable sales tax. Canadian residents will be charged applicable provincial taxes and GST. This offer is limited to one order per household. All orders subject to approval. Credit or debit balances in a customer's account(s) may be offset by any other outstanding balance owed by or to the customer. Please allow 4 to 6 weeks for delivery.

Your Privacy: Harlequin is committed to protecting your privacy. Our Privacy Policy is available online at www.eHarlequin.com or upon request from the Reader Service. From time to time we make our lists of customers available to reputable firms who may have a product or service of interest to you. If you would prefer we not share your name and address, please check here. ☐

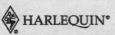

HARLEQUIN®

American **ROMANCE**®

A THREE-BOOK SERIES BY BELOVED AUTHOR

Judy Christenberry

Dallas Duets

**What's behind the doors of
the Yellow Rose Lane apartments?
Love, Texas-style!**

THE MARRYING KIND
May 2007

Jonathan Davis was many things—a millionaire,
a player, a catch. But he'd never be a husband.
For him, "marriage" equaled "mistake." Diane Black
was a forever kind of woman, a babies-and-minivan
kind of woman. But John was confident he could
date her and still avoid that trap.
Until he kissed her...

Also watch for:
DADDY NEXT DOOR
January 2007

MOMMY FOR A MINUTE
August 2007

Available wherever Harlequin books are sold.

www.eHarlequin.com

HARM07JC

nocturne™

IT'S TIME TO DISCOVER THE RAINTREE TRILOGY...

There have always been those among us who are more than human...

Don't miss the dramatic first book by *New York Times* bestselling author

LINDA HOWARD

RAINTREE: *Inferno*

On sale May.

Raintree: Haunted by Linda Winstead Jones
Available June.

Raintree: Sanctuary by Beverly Barton
Available July.